A Candlelight Ecstasy Romance ®

"AS LONG AS MY REPUTATION PRECEDED ME, I DIDN'T WANT TO DISAPPOINT."

His mouth took hers in warm, tender possession as her soul seemed to rush up to meet his. His hands moved over her back, her hips, discovering the soft, feminine contours.

She could feel the thud of his heart against her breasts, and it was as disturbed as hers. She was being made complete, standing there in the darkness, with the water lapping against the shore, experiencing the touch, the kiss of this controlled yet passionate man. She should have pushed him away, but she couldn't—not if her life had depended on it!

A CANDLELIGHT ECSTASY ROMANCE ®

A DANGEROUS HAVEN

Shirley Hart

A CANDLELIGHT ECSTASY ROMANCE ®

Published by
Dell Publishing Co., Inc.
1 Dag Hammarskjold Plaza
New York, New York 10017

Dell ® TM 681510, Dell Publishing Co., Inc.

Candlelight Ecstasy Romance®, 1,203,540,
is a registered trademark of Dell Publishing
Co., Inc., New York, New York.

ISBN: 0-440-12032-2

Printed in the United States of America
First printing—July 1983

To Our Readers:

We have been delighted with your enthusiastic response to Candlelight Ecstasy Romances®, and we thank you for the interest you have shown in this exciting series.

In the upcoming months we will continue to present the distinctive sensuous love stories you have come to expect only from Ecstasy. We look forward to bringing you many more books from your favorite authors and also the very finest work from new authors of contemporary romantic fiction.

As always, we are striving to present the unique, absorbing love stories that you enjoy most—books that are more than ordinary romance.

Your suggestions and comments are always welcome. Please write to us at the address below.

Sincerely,

The Editors
Candlelight Romances
1 Dag Hammarskjold Plaza
New York, New York 10017

CHAPTER ONE

"Your glass is empty again, darling," Eric said, and a frown puckered his brows. "Can I get you another or . . ."

All she would need was another drink and one more selection from that classical pre-Bach *dum-da-dum-da-dum* of lute and recorder album that was on the stereo to put her asleep on her feet. But Tarra Hallworth shrugged and extended her glass to him over the improvised bar. "Yes, please."

In a murmured undertone he said anxiously, "You are enjoying yourself, aren't you?" To her noncommittal half smile he said smugly, "I told you you would. It's time you started getting out. You've been hiding away long enough."

He didn't need to remind her that she hadn't wanted to come to his party for the employees of the gallery. A twenty-nine-year-old lawyer doesn't want to admit to herself that there might be situations she can't handle, but after her divorce, Tarra had become extremely wary of parties. She hadn't wanted to attend, but she had been trapped into coming because she was vacationing next door in her parents' cottage and because she simply couldn't think of a way to put Eric off again. She had done that so many times. . . .

She crossed the room to sink down into a deep, comfortable chair. Dede didn't seem to be bothered by the music. The red-haired girl sat on the floor in front of the fireplace, her legs crossed, her attention on a long-limbed male lying on his stomach beside her. Inwardly Tarra smiled. Dede had tried for ages to attract Vince Malone's interest.

The cottage on Conesus Lake was a perfect setting for a budding romance. A glass wall stretched the length of the room, and though Tarra had her back to it, she knew that the lake was a dark slate color at night and that lights from the opposite shore—yellow, green, and orange—streamed across its mirror stillness.

Out on the patio someone laughed. She turned her drink around in her hand, her coffee-brown hair brushing over her bare shoulders. The sound of that laugh made her feel incredibly lonely. But she had to accept that. She would probably be alone for the rest of her life.

A bottle clinked, drew her eye back to Eric. He smiled at her. He should have been the perfect answer. He was tall, slender, darkly handsome, passionately interested in art—and he had asked her to marry him. She had refused. One week as his wife would have her climbing walls.

A drop of water, condensation from her drink, plopped onto her dress. With an impatient flick of her slender hand she brushed at the skirt of the gauzy ice-blue dress she wore with its ruffles pulled down over her shoulders and frowned in irritation. She was looking at the spot when that shuddery, half-aware feeling crawled down her spine. Someone was staring at her. She raised her head, and her gaze slammed head-on with the vivid green eyes of the guest of honor. He had been backed up against the mantel by Pamela, their resident siren, but he was staring at Tarra. Pamela didn't know a Van Gogh from a Picasso, but she was engaged in a heated conversation with Kaynon Edwards about the value of museums in a community. Kaynon Edwards, Eric's younger brother, the guest of honor. A welcome-home party for the prodigal son. At thirty-two he was an art critic and sports enthusiast, touted by the press as the closest thing to a modern version of the Renaissance man our society would produce. They had also branded him as a womanizer—a man who worked in public relations for museums, theaters, art galleries—and wherever he worked, wealthy women materialized out of nowhere, women who expressed a sudden and avid interest in the repository of art that Kaynon Edwards represented.

In more ways than one.

And now, while Pamela talked to him, he stared at Tarra.

All right, she would play his silly game, she thought, meeting the brazen glance with fire in her own dark eyes. She didn't like him. She hadn't liked him when they were children playing together on the beach, and she didn't like him now. He was far too aware of himself, too male, too good-looking as he stood there, his compact-muscled body leaning against the mantel, a half-consumed drink in his hand, the soft lighting making his dark auburn hair look deep brown, his eyes moving over her seated slender figure, lingering on the high, full curves of her breasts, the rather more generous curves of her hips. She hadn't seen him in years, even though their families were longtime friends, but she admitted she had been prejudiced in advance about him. His reputation in art circles was well known. He spelled success in any fund-raising project— but there was always rampant rumor about his methods for obtaining that success.

She felt a sudden wistful tug, a longing somewhere in the pit of her stomach. Where had that boy gone, the one who swung out from the tree limb over the lake and yelled like Tarzan as he dropped into the water? He might have been a show-off, but she liked him infinitely better than this grown-up version, this devastatingly attractive, auburn-haired lothario, who had a knowing, cynical twist to the full curve of his mouth.

He frowned slightly, as if he had read her thoughts. Then somehow, she wasn't quite sure how, he extracted himself from Pamela's grip on his arm and left her watching with limpid eyes as he strolled toward Tarra's chair, his drink still in his hand.

He was as unconventional in his dress as his life-style. He wore a silk shirt in a dark, brick-red color tucked into his trousers, a shirt that must have been designed especially for his broad shoulders. The opening was not the conventional button-down-the-front kind, but one that buttoned off to the side with the buttons hidden under a placket, like a doctor's. He wore it partially undone so that the material lay back in a triangular flap and exposed a patch of dark, silky hair at the base of his throat. Nestled in it was a carved wooden medallion suspended from a leather thong. The sleeves of the shirt were full, gathered at the wrist, and caught in a cuff. Very few men would have had the nerve or the blatant virility to wear such an unusual style and carry it off with such élan.

"We haven't had a chance to talk, Tarra." His voice was low, attractive, and despite her determination not to react, a nerve quivered somewhere deep within her. She stiffened slightly and strove for a cool look that was polite yet detached, tilting her head to look up at him from her seated position.

"There were others who wanted to talk to you."

The rest of the sentence hung unspoken in the air. He finished it. "And you didn't?"

"I didn't say that," she countered, her voice low.

Undeterred by her lack of enthusiasm, he knelt and sat down on the floor at her feet, crossing his legs easily and tucking them under him. "As good as. I wonder why." One dark auburn brow lifted, and she looked quickly away to avoid meeting that knowing stare. The upward movement of her head caught Eric's eye. He sent her a warm smile. She returned it with such a high-voltage one of her own, Eric looked stunned. Beside her, Kaynon taunted softly, "You have a little something going with my brother?"

She hesitated, then favored her tormentor with a pallid

version of the smile she had flashed at Eric. Antagonistic humor gleamed in the brown depths of her eyes. "I'm not sure what business it is of yours, but to set your mind at ease, I can say quite truthfully that I have no designs on your brother's body—or his money."

"Who said anything about money?" His eyes narrowed as he gazed at her with speculation lighting the dark green depths. "Your parents were well-heeled, as I remember."

She gave him a quick, amused glance. "Then perhaps it's the other way around: Eric is after my money. Are you warning me off?"

"If I am, it has nothing to do with money." He let her absorb that for a moment. Trying not to jump to the obvious conclusion that he was displeased about her friendship with his brother because he was interested in her himself, she frowned. His eyes caught hers and held them as his mouth mocked her. "Do you always equate personal interest with money?"

Before she thought, she said sharply, "I didn't until—" She skidded to a halt.

"Until you married Bryant Reece."

She sat in shocked silence, wondering how he had learned about her marriage, when it had ended so quickly —in less than a year. It had been another year since the final decree. It was as if she had never been married.

"He was ambitious and mercenary, as I remember," Kaynon Edwards said flatly.

"I'd forgotten he was in your class at school." If there was one subject she did not want to talk about, it was her former husband. "You're planning on working for the museum in the city, your father tells me."

He had set his own drink off to the side when he sat down, and now he reached for hers. She had all she could do to keep from flinching away as she felt the lean strength of his fingers closing over her hand. The cool glass underneath and the warmth of his hand on top made her dizzy with a sensation she couldn't define. For one incredible

11

moment she felt as if the essence of him had touched her. Then his hand was gone, carrying the glass to a spot on the soft rug beside his own. "I think you've had enough," he said, ignoring her question about his work.

"You were counting?"

He nodded. "Three. Too many for a woman of your height and weight."

"I'm not a midget—"

"Nor exactly an amazon either." He squinted at her. "You're about five feet five inches tall and weigh a hundred and twenty pounds—give or take a few."

"You missed your calling," she said dryly. "You should work as a cattle buyer."

He gave her an amused sidelong glance. "Buying antiques is like buying cattle. You look at the thing and assess its weight and size in comparison to others in the same category." He paused and then said softly, "But the best test of anything is how it feels when you hold it in your hands . . ." another pause, "whether it's an antique porcelain vase . . . or a woman."

His voice had dropped to a low, intimate level, and his face was close to the knee covered by her gauzy dress. It was as if by talking about holding a woman, he was, in his mind, holding her, exploring her body in the act of love.

Her throat closed. The sounds of the party went on around her, the low murmuring of people's voices, the recorder playing its lilting six-eight rhythm, but the world seemed to skid to a stop and then suddenly resume its orbiting at a newer, faster pace.

This couldn't be happening to her, not again. She was finished with good-looking men who lived by their wits. She had to get up, get away from him, get out in the fresh air and take deep breaths and cleanse these thoughts out of her head.

She made a movement, and he seemed to read her mind. He pushed himself to his feet with a lithe grace and grasped her wrist that lay on the arm of the chair. "Let's go out and look at the lake."

She wanted to resist that tug on her arm, she wanted to tell him no. But she could feel the hard determination in his grip, and she knew that any resistance on her part would simply put her at his mercy more than ever. Those fingers clamped around her revealed the hard ruthlessness that lay under the cynical charm.

The swish of the sliding glass door sent her skirt billowing around her, flattening it against her hips and thighs. Once they were out on the deck, though, the breeze shifted and her skirt blew upward. She pressed it down with her arms and walked quickly to the edge of the deck to lean against the railing, acutely aware of Kaynon standing beside her, looking into her burning face.

"Are you really that embarrassed because the wind showed me a glimpse of your lovely legs—or are you angry because I strong-armed you out here?"

She turned to face him, the railing supporting her hip. "Look, I'm sure you must find it amusing to tease the little girl you played with once, but I don't find it so funny." She turned and gestured at the place where the lake lapped against the shore just under the edge of the deck. "A lot of water has, as they say, touched the sands of time, or something like that."

He reached out and touched her cheek with his fingertip. "You've got your metaphors mixed."

She moved away. "Don't—touch me."

"How many?" he murmured softly, his hand dropping away.

"What?" She faced him, moving her head slightly to let the breeze blow her hair away from her cheek.

"How many layers of hurt and anger and frustration will I have to cut through?"

"None," she said, her voice crisp. "I'm healing nicely, thank you, and without your help."

"Who is helping you? My brother?"

She was furious now. His cool, male assumption that she needed a man to cure her made her say in a barely controlled fury, "This may come as a surprise, but I am a practicing lawyer and find the work both exhausting and therapeutic, and far better for my ego than a night in bed with some man who couldn't care less what happens to me when I wake up in the morning." She took a breath and then plunged on. "So if you're thinking of adding me to your countrywide harem, you can forget it. I liked you better when you just sounded like Tarzan and didn't act like him!"

She made a move as if to walk past him, but he was too quick for her. "What in the hell are you talking about? What has my brother been telling you?"

She opened her mouth to tell him that she had other friends in the art circle, but something stopped her. She didn't have to excuse herself to him. If he began to hate her, so much the better. Then she would be safe. . . .

"Your brother told me nothing. Your reputation is well known, and if I hadn't already heard about you, seeing is believing."

He didn't betray himself by answering her. He simply moved with the speed of a striking cobra, grasped her, and pulled her into his arms. His mouth took hers in a warm, tender possessiveness that seemed to draw her soul up to meet his. His hands moved over her back, her hips, discovering the soft, feminine contours.

She should have pushed him away, but she couldn't. She was being made complete, standing there in that soft dark, with the water lapping against the shore, experiencing the touch and kiss of this controlled yet passionate man. She could feel the thud of his heart against her breasts, and it was as disturbed as hers. She couldn't have pushed him away if her life had depended upon it. Instead, her arms and hands were molding his back, feeling the hard flesh under silk with a pleasure that had nothing to do with aesthetics. It was the primitive pleasure of a woman touching a man.

He lifted his mouth and murmured, "As long as my reputation preceded me—I didn't want to disappoint." He looked down at her pale, upturned face. "Are you angry?"

She realized she was still holding his back with a grip that was equal to his when he escorted her outside. She dropped her hands at once. "No." Her sense of humor and proportion reasserted itself. "How could I be angry? I didn't exactly fight you off." She felt dazed—as if he had possessed her.

He smiled, and that flash of white teeth in the darkness did something to her already unstable heart. "No, you didn't, did you? I would almost say you enjoyed it as much as I did." He leaned forward and kissed her on the nose, a light brush of the lips that still had the power to distort reality.

"Tarra? Are you out here?"

It was Eric, and, somehow, she was annoyed rather than relieved. "Over here, Eric."

Kaynon still held her, keeping his arm around her waist and locking her to his side as she turned to face Eric. She knew the elder brother couldn't see that hand on her side, but she could feel every finger through her dress as if they were branded on her flesh, and her cheeks burned. It wouldn't take a genius to guess that Kaynon had been kissing her on the dark patio.

Eric's face was shadowed, but his voice seemed normal enough. "Enjoying the view?" There was a faint edge of challenge in his voice.

Kaynon didn't answer. Tarra, unable to step free of his grip without revealing how tightly he held her, stayed where she was and said lightly, "We were recalling old times—when the three of us played here. Do you remember, Eric?"

He was silent for a moment and then said, "I remember

how Mother was always telling me not to strain myself trying to keep up with you."

"But she was right to be concerned," Tarra said lightly. "You can't fault her for that. You haven't had any trouble since, have you?"

"No, my rheumatic heart and I have come to a truce of sorts," Eric said easily. Even in the dark, Tarra could see Eric's eyes drift over the more muscular physique of his brother. "As long as I don't try to be athlete of the year, I'm okay." He took a step forward and said, "Can I get you another drink or anything?"

"She's had enough." Kaynon's voice was crisp.

Eric looked at him, his mouth curved in amusement. "She doesn't have to drive back to the city."

Kaynon's grip on her waist tightened. "Is she staying . . . with you?"

Eric smiled. "I wish she were, but no, on two counts. I have to get back to the city tonight, and she's vacationing here in her family's cottage—next door. She'll be your neighbor for the next two weeks, Kaynon."

His grip relaxed, and his fingers moved up and down the seam of her dress, sensuously exploring that sensitive bare area under her arm. "Really?" He glanced down at her and smiled. "Well, well, well. That's good news. I wonder why you didn't mention that."

"I—didn't know you were staying at the lake, too." And she hadn't. It was enough to send a little pulse of alarm beating along her veins.

"I don't have an apartment," he said in explanation, "and I didn't want to move in with Dad and Eric—at least not until I've looked for a place somewhere else."

There were cottonwoods growing next to the shore all around the lake, and the deck had one growing straight up through the center of it. Rather than cut the tree down, the Edwardses had simply built the deck around it. The wind rattled the papery leaves of that tree together, and Eric walked over to lean against the trunk and look out

16

over the lake. He had purposely removed himself from them and was viewing them out of the corner of his eye with a cool detachment. Tarra could see the outline of his white hand against the dark bark. "You're lucky, Kaynon," he said softly. "I envy you your view," he kept his eyes focused on the lake, "but I don't envy your having to get up at five o'clock to drive into the city."

"I'll survive. I'll just have to go to bed earlier, that's all."

"Yes, I suppose you will. There won't be the . . . distractions out here that there are in the city—at least," looking at Tarra, "I hope there aren't."

The sudden tenseness in Kaynon's muscles communicated itself to every nerve in hers. "Don't bait me, Brother."

Eric looked at him then. "I wouldn't dream of it, Brother."

The hostility sang between them like a fine wire drawn at high tension. Tarra moved restlessly, and all at once Kaynon's hand fell away and she was free. To Eric, she said, "Are you planning to serve coffee soon? I'll be glad to help you if you are."

"Yes, perhaps it is time. I'd appreciate your help," Eric said in a soft voice, and it was as if the ugly words of a moment ago didn't exist. She took a step, and Kaynon said softly, "Perhaps I can help, too?"

"I wouldn't ask you to do that," Eric said smoothly. "You're the guest of honor."

The brightly lit kitchen seemed like a relief to her heated skin, her jarred nerves. Eric gave her instructions, and while he made the coffee, she prepared the food for the cold buffet—slices of ham and Swiss cheese, cold meat loaf and pickle loaf and Muenster. She arranged slices of thick wheat bread and the rye that was a favorite of Eric's on a tray and found the mustard and mayonnaise containers in the refrigerator and carried them through to the dining room.

17

When she returned, Eric said to her softly, "You will be careful, won't you, darling? Don't get involved with Kaynon. He's a devil with women, and he has no regard for their feelings at all. I've seen him walk away from a woman who had done everything for him—without a backward glance."

"I . . . appreciate your concern. But my love life is my own affair, surely."

He laughed, but there was little amusement in the sound. "I suppose it is your own 'affair', as you so aptly put it. Just watch out for my lethal brother. They should put a sign on him. 'Beware, destructive to women.' "

"If you believe that, you don't know women at all. He'd be even more attractive to them."

He put the coffee carafe under the automatic drip maker and turned to give her an enigmatic look. "You must be right. I don't know women at all . . . because I'd swear you'd be the last one he could successfully entice out to the patio for a little kissing session."

Her cheeks flooded with color. She lifted her head, her whole body stiffening with resentment and anger. "You have no right to tell me what to do."

He took a step toward her, but he didn't touch her. "I've asked you to be my wife."

"And I told you it was out of the question."

"Believe me, I'm only trying to protect you. I have to tell you the truth about that man, even if he is my own brother. He has no scruples where women are concerned, none at all. He uses their money and he uses their bodies, and when he's done with them, he tosses them away."

"Into the Genessee River?" she asked dryly, trying to strive for a sense of reality to deter him from his dramatic denunciation of his brother.

"No, of course not." Eric was impatient. He did not want to be deterred. "He isn't that stupid."

"Eric." She laid her hand on his arm and tried not to compare the flaccid muscles beneath the skin with those

18

of the man she had just kissed. "I appreciate your concern, honestly I do. But, really, does it seem likely that I'll fall into your brother's arms after what I went through with my—with Bryant?"

"Still trying to administer the antidote against my fatal charm, Brother?" Kaynon leaned in the doorway, his mouth twisted.

Now Eric was the one who was determined to lighten the mood. He flashed his younger brother a smile. "Absolutely. I'm doing the best I can. And I'm succeeding." He smiled down at Tarra. The sudden change of attitude was calculated, it had to be. Eric did not want to appear to be the staid elder brother to her.

"Well," Kaynon drawled, "since she's now been immunized, she can eat with me." He grasped her elbow and said, "You've been in the kitchen long enough. Humor the guest of honor."

She might have known it wouldn't be simple to walk away from him. But she wasn't going to be the bone of contention between them. If Eric thought he could tell her what to do, he needed to be shown differently, and it certainly wouldn't harm Kaynon Edwards's ego if she could prove to him that she could be in his company without being swept off her feet.

"I'd be delighted," she said, unable to look back over her shoulder and see the expression on Eric's face, much as she wanted to. But the mocking, sardonic smile that barely hid Kaynon's surprise was reward enough.

Dede and Vince and Pamela and the man she had found to replace Kaynon followed them, moving around the table to make their sandwiches. Holding her plate and a steaming cup of coffee, Tarra went into the living room and sat down on the floor in front of the fire. Kaynon settled in next to her.

The fire snapped and crackled. A little blue crown of flame leapt above the logs, and the pungent smell of burning applewood filled her nose. Bruce Edwards, Kaynon and Eric's father, had hired a man to cut down an old apple tree on the cottage property last fall, and it was that tree that burned in front of her, a tree she had climbed as a child. But that was the way of life; things changed and people changed. . . .

"You look very pensive."

"I'm sorry," she told Kaynon, turning to smile at him. "I'm not exactly what you had in mind for a dinner companion, am I?"

She turned her head and went back to staring into the fire. He put his plate down as if he had suddenly lost his appetite and caught her elbow to turn her toward him. "Look, if I'm getting in the way, if you've really got something good going with Eric, I'll bow out of the picture."

She stared at him and wondered if the fire was playing tricks on her, making her see the leap of a dark emotion flickering in the depths of his peculiar slate-green eyes. Here was not the womanizer, the manipulator of women. Here was a warm, caring man, a man who didn't want to cause her pain or humiliation. Something about him—his eyes, the way his hand was holding her arm—made her realize that at this particular moment the guard was down. She was seeing Kaynon Edwards as few women saw him —open . . . and vulnerable. He wanted the truth even if it hurt. And that was it, the thing that mystified her. If she said she preferred Eric, he would be hurt. But he would keep his word, he would get up and walk away without a backward glance. And somehow, she knew that would hurt *her*.

"I was thinking about that tree," she said, watching him, tilting her head toward the fireplace so that he would understand what she was talking about. "And how I used to climb it."

He searched her face for a moment, and then released his grip on her elbow and smiled slightly. "Were you?" He picked up his plate again and began to eat, as if her oblique answer had satisfied him completely.

"Tell me about your work," she said, suddenly wanting to know. "Are you planning on having a fund-raising drive for the gallery?"

He shook his head. "No, not right now. My father is mostly interested in expanding community participation. He and Eric have been at loggerheads about it for months. Eric doesn't want people tramping about, messing up his beautiful gallery. Dad feels there should be more traffic through. He hates the fact that Eric's charging admission, but there's not a lot he can do about it. Funds are low everywhere. Government sources are drying up, and there simply aren't as many wealthy people who are willing to contribute to the arts. I read in the paper the other day about some man who gave a half million dollars to an engineering college." Kaynon shrugged. "The college had given him his degree, made it possible for him to earn that money. Why shouldn't he return the favor? But on the other hand, the arts have a place in everyone's life, even if one isn't an artist or a sculptor. But if we try to keep the gallery the way Eric wants it to be—an exclusive little sanctuary—we shouldn't be surprised if the city turns a deaf ear when we ask for money."

He shrugged. "I'm not saying that's been the case entirely. As chairman of the gallery board, Dad wields a lot of influence, and he's been doing a creditable job of giving the gallery visibility and making it attractive to all different kinds of people. The art show draws thousands, and it's held on the gallery grounds; so at least once a year people are forced to drive downtown and find it, anyway." He stared into the fire. "There's just so much competition for people's time and money. Movies, theater, dinner out—" he raked a hand through his hair. "God! People must eat out every Friday night. I made the mistake of trying to eat out last week. So it isn't that people don't have money or can't get out." He looked at her and gave a self-deprecatory grin. "Sorry. You did ask, you know."

21

She smiled. "You forget. I've known your father for years."

"And heard the same things said over and over. I'm sorry if I've bored you to death—"

"You haven't. As it happens, I agree with you."

"And are you a regular visitor?"

She hesitated, considered lying, and then said softly, "No . . . not now."

"Why not?"

"I . . . have my reasons." She couldn't tell him the truth, that she avoided the gallery because of Eric.

"And I'd say at a guess those reasons have nothing to do with art." He was perceptive and entirely too quick. *An all-around dangerous man, Mr. Kaynon Edwards.*

"I was busy working for several years, and I got out of the habit, I suppose," she said casually.

"You're not interested in the arts?" He pressed her deeper into the lie. She had to tell the truth and yet somehow avoid giving herself away. She wasn't ready to expose her inner life, her soul, to a man again. She wouldn't be ready for years.

"Yes, I am, but—"

"They aren't a part of your life."

She stared at him, knowing she should tell him the truth, but that need to protect an important part of herself from him made her say carefully, "The arts are as much a part of my life as—as anyone else's, I suppose." She didn't cross her fingers, but she had an idiotic urge to do so.

"Look, what are you doing now?"

She gave him a startled look, and he said, "No, I don't mean right now, I mean during the next week or so. You're on vacation, Eric said?"

She nodded and tried to think how to put him off tactfully. "My first year in practice was hectic. I've been hoping to just soak up some sun and catch up on my reading—legal and pleasure."

"Good, then your schedule is pretty free. We'll set a day and I'll give you a grand tour. You might be surprised at some of the things Eric has acquired."

"I'm not sure—"

"No more excuses, Tarra. You and I have a date." He smiled then, a long, slow smile, and she knew she had made a grave tactical error in underestimating this man. Even at her age, knowing what he was, she was no more immune to his charisma than the most naive young woman.

They talked about other things after that, she wasn't sure what. Her mind seemed to dwell on one thing—escape. She accomplished it later, by getting to her feet, taking her plate out into the kitchen, and telling Eric she was going home. It was one of the luxuries she granted herself now, going home from a party when she felt like it. No more waiting about for Bryant to make that final contact, leave that one lasting impression.

"I'll walk you home," Eric said after she told him she was leaving.

"Don't be ridiculous. It's all of thirty feet. Stay here and keep your guests happy."

She walked through the hall into the bedroom where she had laid her shawl, and on the way out the door she heard Pamela's voice—and Kaynon's low, attractive tones, saying something in reply.

The screen door gave its familiar creak as she propped it open and unlocked the inside door. She flipped on a light and then turned on the stairway light and turned off the kitchen light before she began to climb the stairs—alone.

Some people said the mornings were worst, but she could cope with the mornings. Mornings brought daylight and breakfast to make and a day to look forward to. Nighttimes were the worst. At night she forgot the quarrels, the viciousness and remembered only the warm comfort of Bryant's body in the bed next to hers.

She pulled down the shade, undressed, and got into her

sheer white nightgown. With the light off she raised the shade to open the window and let in the cool night breeze. The Edwards's cottage was blazing with light at every window, and she could see the flicker of the fire in the fireplace, even though she couldn't see into the living room. But the kitchen was on the near side of the house. Framed in the window, the light from the overhead fixture gleaming on his auburn hair, stood Kaynon, his arms around Pamela's waist. She saw them as clearly as if they were standing in a spotlight. Pamela was so close to him that her breasts were pressed against the brick-red shirt, and Kaynon had that bored, rather cynical look on his face that was already beginning to be familiar.

She caught her breath. As if he had heard her, he looked up, and as he stared at the darkened window, his expression changed, became hard, purposeful. She shrank back, knowing that her guilty conscience was making a fool of her. He couldn't have seen her. It was almost impossible to see out into the dark from a lighted window. She would get into bed. What difference did it make whether he kissed Pamela? It was none of her business.

Then why was she still standing there? And worse, why was she leaning forward, straining to see? She wished she hadn't. For Kaynon was no longer looking up. He was lowering his head toward Pamela, placing his mouth over her full lips.

CHAPTER TWO

When she woke up, she had a headache. She hadn't slept
well. And Kaynon Edwards was there, inside her head, as
he had been all night. She fixed coffee and tidied the
cottage, restlessly folding newspapers and straightening
the cover on the couch, willing him out of her mind.

The cottage was comfortable but not elegant. Her parents used bamboo furniture and area rugs to keep mainte-
nance at a minimum and ward off mildew—that
ever-present annoyance that was the price of waterfront
living. She vacuumed and dusted, chores that took her all
of twenty minutes, and looked at the stack of reading she
meant to do before she returned to the hectic routine of
the office. She doubted if she could concentrate on any of
it. Dressed in brief shorts and a halter top, she walked up
to the little store for the milk she needed. The cottage next
door was quiet.

Back in the living room, she took out her writing case
and wrote a letter to her parents, one they would find
waiting at home for them when they returned from their
trip to Europe. She walked out to the mailbox, put the
letter inside, raised the red flag, and went back into the
house.

By noon she was ready to put on her swimsuit and go
lie out on the dock. There was still no movement or life
next door. Perhaps Kaynon was no longer there. Perhaps
one kiss had not been enough. Perhaps he had gone back
with Pamela to the city to spend the night with her.

She shut out the mental pictures that rose in her mind and went up to her bedroom to put on her suit. It was a white maillot, cut so high over her hips it exposed her hipbones. Purchased a year ago when her confidence in herself as a woman had been at a very low ebb, the suit gave her a long, lean look and did great things for her bustline. She already had a light, golden tan.

She faced the mirror, knowing that she looked the best she had looked in several years. Promising herself she would protect her long brown hair with a towel when she was out in the sun, she rubbed a light suntan oil into her skin. With protective gloss on her lips, she picked up the towel, a historical romance she was certain would not have a single legal term in it, and a lounge cushion, and let herself out the porch door.

The lake was a beautiful deep blue, a reflection from the blue sky above. The white wisps of clouds were no threat of rain. A narrow "finger" lake, Conesus was less than a mile wide, and she gazed across at the opposite shore and could see the houses sitting next to each other, their windows all facing out toward the water. It was pleasant here, and she meant to enjoy it no matter who took up residence next door or swam from the dock that was next to hers. She couldn't let Kaynon Edwards spoil what she had hoped would be a restful, refreshing break from work.

At the end of the dock she settled her sunglasses on her nose, stretched out on her stomach on the long cushion, propped her chin in her elbows, and began to read. The story was a good one and got her involved right from the first page, something that didn't always happen.

Had she been subconsciously waiting for the sound of steps on the dock next to hers? She lay there and suddenly the words blurred and began to run together. They made no sense. She was straining to hear. Then she realized how ridiculous she was being. He would certainly notice her lack of response. The normal thing to do was to turn, wave casually, and go back to her reading.

She turned her head just in time to see him do a shallow dive off the dock. Broad shoulders, lean hips clad in a brief dark blue swimsuit, muscular arms arrowed over his head, he sliced through the water and was several feet out when he began to swim.

There was no danger in being caught watching him now. Facedown, he was moving at racing speed, doing a classic crawl with arms bent, feet churning, turning his head out for a breath on every fourth stroke. It was like watching a human torpedo. He had launched himself toward the middle of the lake and kept to his course. She wondered if he might be trying to go the length. To do so was dangerous and foolhardy without a boat as an escort. Surely he must know he ran the risk of being run down by a careless speedboat driver, particularly on a warm, cloudless Saturday afternoon like this one. There weren't many people out yet, it was true, but in another hour the lake would be churning with boats crossing and recrossing its ten-mile length and one-mile width. She was wondering what luck she would have if she stood up and tried to call him back, when he turned suddenly and began to swim toward the shore.

She relaxed and forced her eyes down to her book, but the words that had been so absorbing a moment ago seemed meaningless. As she had last night, she relived that moment in his arms. Why had he kissed her? And why had she responded? She hadn't felt that swift rush of passion with any man since Bryant. But hard on the heels of her memory of his kiss was the mental picture of Pamela in his arms, the dark auburn head lowering to those full, red lips—cool drops of water scattered over her heated back brought a sharp exclamation to her lips. "Oh!" She sat up and crossed her legs under her, peering at the sky, wondering how it could be raining with the sun shining so brightly.

"Good afternoon."

Like some predatory shark he had glided underwater

27

and come up beside the dock to spatter her. Now he was standing at knee depth in front of her, white teeth glistening as he smiled at her.

She thought of those arms clasping Pamela and said coolly, "At least it was."

Her rudeness amused him. "What happened to change it?"

She looked at him. "You happened."

Unperturbed he flattened his palms on the dock and swung himself up to sit beside her. That six square feet of space suddenly shrank. Water from his body dripped over her. "Do you mind?" Her voice was icy.

"What's the matter, Tarra? Didn't you get enough sleep last night?"

From his sitting position he picked up the suntan lotion and unscrewed the cap of the bottle. She watched, incredibly aware of the male, virile attraction of him. The hair that she had glimpsed at his throat arrowed down his chest to disappear under the line of his swimming trunks. The shoulders that she had guessed at being broad and muscular were definitely so. His skin had a light, allover tan that didn't seem to stop at his waistline.

Thinking he was going to spread her suntan lotion on his body and knowing how she would feel watching him do it, she clasped her crossed legs in front of her and said, "Has it occurred to you to buy your own?"

"It occurred to me. But I decided it wasn't a good idea."

But he didn't rub the lotion on himself. Instead, he readjusted his position and leaned behind her. She felt the palm of his hand on her back before she realized what he intended to do. She wanted to cry out and push his hand away, but she knew that was exactly what he expected her to do. He was playing a game with her, and her only defense was to pretend that his touch didn't affect her. If she could keep from betraying how much his warm hand on her naked back disturbed her, she would know her acting skills were as good as any trial lawyer's.

He started at her shoulders, his palm working the lotion in, his fingers smooth and slick as they moved over her naked back. She clenched her teeth and told herself he was no different from any other man and his touch meant nothing to her, but her suit was cut low, nearly to the base of her spine, and when she had almost convinced herself she was winning, his hand wandered down and slowly massaged the sensitive hollow of her back.

Her willpower failed her. "That's enough," she said sharply.

His fingers drifted over the very lowest point of her spine and then moved away. "I wonder why you're so angry with me today," he murmured, an amused lilt in his voice. "Last night we seemed to be on more—friendly terms."

"Perhaps it's seeing you in the cold light of day," she retorted.

"It's not cold. I can feel how warm the sun has made your skin . . ."

He moved his hand to the nape of her neck, found the bony outline of her spine, and let his fingers trail down the long, lotion-slick length to the erogenous base. There, he toyed with the edge of her suit as if he were considering insinuating his fingertips under the satiny material.

She sat utterly still, knowing her only defense was a pretended lack of response. If she could keep from betraying the leap of reaction under her skin, he would give up his sensual seduction. But he didn't. His hand moved to her left thigh and traced around the line of her suit leg up to the top of her exposed hipbone, his cool green gaze watching her. On that sensitive spot, he rotated his fingertips in a slow, circular motion.

Every nerve cell in her body quivered. Her willpower collapsed, and her temper exploded into heated rage. "Take your hands off me. Save your caresses and your kisses for Pamela. She's more your type." She pulled her legs under her to get to her feet—but with lightning quickness he grabbed her shoulders and her thighs, and in the next instant she was lying on her back on the cushion, and he was leaning over her, her wrists shackled by his hands.

And he was smiling.

"Now we're getting somewhere," he breathed, and she knew at once that her response to his touch had stamped-ed her into making a serious error. He murmured, "That *was* you at the window last night, wasn't it?"

She didn't even consider lying. He was bent over her, watching her like a hawk, his eyes on her pupils, his hands at the pulse points of her wrists. He was a human lie detector. "Yes."

"You were watching me kiss Pamela."

"Yes," she said again, watching his eyes flare with satis-faction at the breathy sound of her affirmative answer.

Then he administered the coup de grace. "And you were jealous."

She stared back at those green eyes. His head seemed to obscure everything. He loomed in front of her like a giant screen blowup, and she saw every detail of his face—the smooth jaw recently shaved, the dark sideburns even dark-er with moisture, the elegant long nose. "Yes," she breathed, knowing that even the slightest attempt to lie would be immediately obvious to him.

"Now we *are* getting somewhere," he murmured. He lowered his head, and she shut her eyes, the sweet agony of waiting almost more than she could bear.

He didn't make her wait long. He seemed to share her impatience. The warm urgency in his mouth made his kiss just as devastating as it had been last night—more so, because now he was kissing her as he lay half sprawled over her and she could feel the weight of his chest on her breasts, the bump of his hipbone against hers, the hard muscles of his thigh on hers. It was as if her subconscious had been serving up the look and feel of Kaynon's mouth and body all night long and she was powerless to deny the yearning of those hidden dreams. She lifted her arms and

30

clasped his cool, wet shoulders, stroked the damp hair at his nape. It was like sleek satin to the touch. Her mouth opened and welcomed him, and her tongue touched his.

He shuddered and drew away. "Have a heart, woman. Don't do that to me out here in the wide open spaces."

He leaned over her, and she realized that she still had her hands clasped around his neck. She pulled them away and tried to sit up, but he had braced his palms against the dock on each side of her and she bumped into the solid wall of his chest.

"No," he said softly. "This morning I'm not going to let you run away from me."

She lay back down, her eyes flickering upward. He was amused and aroused, she could see it in his eyes; he wasn't bothering to hide it. There were half a dozen other things hidden in those green depths she didn't even want to think about. Desperate to put him off, she said the first thing that came into her head. "You know what happens when a man kisses the girl next door."

His eyes flickered with lazy amusement. In a studied theatrical tone of the straight man delivering his line, he looked her in the eye and said, "No, Tarra. What happens when a man kisses the girl next door?"

She held his gaze without wavering. "She traps him into marriage with her feminine wiles—or her apple pie."

He threw back his head and laughed—a reaction that was not what she had hoped for. She lifted herself on her elbow, hoping to escape him while he was laughing, but he was too alert for her and nudged her back to the cushion even while he was still chuckling.

Leaning over her, his face wreathed in amusement and something else she couldn't put a name to, he said softly, "Which method have you chosen, neighbor?"

She stared back at him. "If I told you, that would be giving you an unfair advantage, wouldn't it?"

He smiled, his teeth white against his tanned face.

31

"Lady, I have a feeling that with you I'm going to need all the advantages I can get."

He leaned toward her, and the gleam in his eye told her he meant to kiss her again. Panicked, knowing how she would respond to a second onslaught of that warm mouth, she put her palms on his chest and pushed at him. "Kaynon—don't. I—I'm not sure I can handle this right now. I . . . need time." Oh, God, what a lie. He felt so good under her hands, his muscles full and hard, the skin smooth and cool and crisp with hair.

But for once he seemed to be reading her words instead of her body. His eyes wandered over her face. "All right. I can understand that. We need some time to get reacquainted, anyway." He looked at her for a moment and then said softly, "Have dinner with me."

"Tonight?"

For the first time he seemed impatient. "Yes, of course, tonight. There must be some nice places to eat down here."

"There are, but—"

He leaned forward and covered her mouth with his. Even that short contact shook her. "I know," he said, smiling. "You don't have a thing to wear." The smile broadened. "I won't mind. We'll go as we are."

"There are laws about that sort of thing," she reminded him.

"You would think of that." He tilted his head and gave her a considering look. "Shall we eat in?"

"I'm a terrible cook."

He raised an eyebrow and drawled, "Well, I won't have to worry about the apple pie gambit then, will I?"

A heat warmed her cheeks that had nothing to do with the temperature. "Look, just forget I said that, will you? It was just a joke, and I—"

"You were protecting yourself," he said easily, "something you have a perfect right to do. I was pushing too hard. I promise to back off and start over." He lifted his hands. She was free.

"Now, about dinner?"

She got that peculiar feeling again, that he was warm and real and vulnerable and if she said no, he would not only be disappointed, he would be hurt. She had a strange reluctance to hurt him. "I—all right."

Not one of those dark auburn eyelashes flickered. "What time shall I pick you up?"

She thought quickly and said, "How does seven thirty sound?"

"Just right."

He got to his feet, and she sat up and stared at him. She couldn't see his face. He was a dark silhouette against the sun. Whatever was in his eyes was lost to her. "Don't get a sunburn," he said in a bland voice and strolled away from her down the dock.

There were burns and there were burns, she thought ruefully, and Kaynon Edwards was a one-way ticket to a third-degree roasting. That compact, lithe male body moved away from her, every inch of him well shaped even viewed from the rear, broad shoulders tapered to narrow waist, firm-muscled buttocks and thighs. Somehow even the curve of his calves was pleasing, and so was the way he walked with a sort of rolling ease.

Good God, she was thinking like a lovesick teen-ager in the throes of a first crush. She tore her eyes away from him and turned around to stretch out on her stomach again, but the sun beat down on her back, and all she could think about was the way his hands had moved over her skin.

That feeling of nervous excitement didn't leave, even after she had plunged into the cool lake and taken a long swim. The hours seemed to drag until it was time to get ready. Of Kaynon she had seen nothing.

The lake had left a residue in her hair, and she spent a good half hour in the shower sudsing it away. While the water poured over her, she thought about what she would wear. She had brought one dressy dress down, she wasn't sure just why, except that she had learned to pack a basic wardrobe and she had automatically followed that rule when she had packed to come to the cottage. It was an outrageously sexy dress, in a soft cocoa-brown color that matched her hair. Out of the shower, dried and powdered, she took it from the closet and put it on. The bodice was very full at the shoulders and had long sleeves, but it was cut so low that the folds of fabric fell into a draped, narrow opening that didn't stop until near indecency just above her waist. A strip of beige lace bordered the opening of tanned, satiny flesh and lay against the gentle rise of her breasts. The skirt was full and swishy, to just below her knees. She slipped into hose and high strappy sandals, brushed her hair out over her shoulders, and used gold eye shadow to bring out her eyes. She highlighted her lips with a gleamy gloss and added the final touch, a drop of expensive perfume on the insides of her wrists and between her breasts.

You wouldn't feel so safe if he hadn't already promised to hold off, she told the provocative face and body that stared back at her from the mirror, and never stopped to wonder why she believed him implicitly.

Promptly at seven thirty he knocked on her door. She opened it, to find him dressed quite conventionally in a dark suit—but the shirt he wore with it was a pale lemon color, and rather than a tie, he simply wore it open, showing a small, intricately hammered gold figure of a horse hanging from a narrow gold chain nestled in the auburn hair at the base of his throat. The effect was devastating.

His eyes moved over her. He didn't say or do anything exactly, but he seemed to withdraw slightly, and she wondered if she had at last stumbled on the secret of discouraging him, dressing in such a blatantly sexy dress. Did he feel threatened?

To fill in the awkward silence, she said, "Would you like to come in for a drink? I have wine or Scotch—"

He gave her a saturnine look that said volumes and told her how wrong she was about his reaction to her appearance. "I think with you looking like that, we'd better skip the drink and just get in the car."

She had disturbed him then, so much so that he had tried to hide it from her. A forbidden chill feathered over her skin, three parts delight and three parts fear. "You don't like my dress?" She shouldn't court danger this way, but it had been so long since she had seen that flare of desire in a man's eyes—and felt the answering warming in her own body.

"I refuse to answer on the grounds that it may tend to incriminate me, counselor," he said in a low mock growl and took her elbow to guide her out to the car.

He installed her in a shiny dark gray Volkswagen Rabbit. The small car seemed even smaller when he slid into the seat beside her. Out on the road he turned the car south. She asked, "Where are we going?"

"To the Loganberry Barn if that meets with your approval. Know anything about it?"

She shook her head. "It's fairly new. I hear it serves great country French cuisine. It stood empty for several years. I can remember looking at that barn and thinking it had great possibilities. It was an ice cream place for a while and then a pizza parlor. It was remodeled a year or two ago, and now with the thruway open, it caters strictly to dinner clientele."

She sounded like a tour guide. Why was she chattering? She couldn't let his nearness and the pungent, heady scent of his cologne affect her like this.

"Nice to be brought up to date," he murmured, which could have meant nothing—or everything. He was silent then, and she searched her mind for a topic of conversation. It was rather odd, really. She knew him—and yet she didn't.

"Enjoy your swim?" he said suddenly, a mocking note on the edge of his voice.

Determined not to let him undermine her confidence, she answered coolly, "Yes, I did," and tried not to think about him watching her without her knowing. She had a distinct memory of climbing out on the dock and arching her body backward as she rubbed her hair dry. . . .

"You swim well."

"Is there any reason I shouldn't?"

"Somehow I seem to remember you as a pudgy little girl who paddled around the edges and was afraid to go out over her head."

"That's flattering," she said dryly. "I must have been all of ten."

"Well, you obviously aren't pudgy anymore," a quick, cursory sidelong glance, "but I think you still like to play it safe and stay in the shallows, don't you?"

She knew he wasn't talking about swimming, and it annoyed her. "Do you make it a habit of baiting the women you take out for the evening?"

He made a grimace, and under the expensive material of his suit, his shoulders lifted. "No." He drove in silence for a few minutes and then in a rather crisp tone asked, "Have you been to this place with Reece?"

Startled, she turned to look at him. "No. Why do you ask?"

"Because I'm filled with the very normal male urge to take you out to dinner without having to combat the image of another man inside your head."

"We all carry other people inside our heads," she shot back, annoyed. "Certainly an experienced man like yourself has realized that."

"So I have," he murmured. "But sometimes I wonder what makes you think you know me so well. I thought a man was innocent until proven guilty."

Caught, she retreated. "Yes, that's what I was taught in law school."

He didn't drive fast, but they were passing the sign shaped like a barn, turning into the drive and crunching

36

over the gravel, just as she was frantically trying to re-member what courses she had taken, in case he asked.

They climbed the outside stairway, and he put his hand at the back of her waist as any normally polite escort would have done, but those lean, well-shaped fingers seemed to burn through the thin material of her dress, and she remembered the way he had caressed her side the night before. Was he worried about other men inside her head? He didn't need to be. She was aware of every move-ment of his body, the way he leaned forward to open the door for her, the effortless way he guided her through the entryway.

The inside was softly lit, intimate. The high, curved wooden walls did not disguise the fact that they had stepped into a remodeled barn and were walking on the second story of what was surely once the haymow. At the curved ends, two long, narrow windows were filled with the green leaves and twisted branches of the tall trees that surrounded the place and gave her the feeling of being inside an aquarium, looking out.

They were shown to a table near the wall by a petite young woman in a white scoop-necked blouse and black pants, her hair tied back in a long, sleek curl. She handed them the silver menus and asked their preference for a cocktail.

"I'll have a gin and tonic," Tarra told her.

"Dewar's," Kaynon said, "on the rocks."

The waitress looked at him, evident admiration in her glance. She leaned across the table to light the small hurri-cane lamp, turning slightly toward him, and the ruffled neckline of her blouse fell forward a fraction of an inch. Tarra moved restlessly in her chair, and Kaynon's eyes lifted to her face—and stayed there. He seemed more interested in the gleam of antagonism in her eyes than in taking advantage of what was being offered so enticingly to him.

When the waitress left them, he leaned back. "Is something wrong?"

"I'm beginning to think you're a menace, Mr. Edwards," she murmured. "Maybe your brother was right."

Long, brazenly dark-red lashes flickered over his eyes. "And what did my charming brother tell you about me?"

She hesitated. "Nothing, really." She picked up the menu and tried to focus her concentration on it.

Before Kaynon could question her further, the waitress reappeared with their drinks and asked if they had decided what they'd like for dinner. They ordered surf and turf, which gave the petite waitress another opportunity to give Kaynon a perky smile and say softly, "Help yourself—to the salad bar." She gave him another long, interested look before she turned to walk away.

He lifted the short, chunky glass to his lips. "What kind of law do you practice, Tarra?"

"I—work in an office with three other lawyers," she hedged. "Carson, Reynolds, and Taylor."

"Don't you specialize? Are you a trial lawyer?"

She smiled. "Nothing so glamorous. Shall we?" she said, nodding her head toward the buffet table.

There was crispy lettuce and carrot sticks and bean sprouts and bean salad and macaroni and potato salad and grainy brown bread with whipped butter. She was helping herself to the creamy Roquefort dressing, extremely conscious of Kaynon standing just behind her, waiting, when she heard the click of high heels progress down the aisle between the tables, and the throaty sound of a familiar feminine voice she remembered from last night.

"Kaynon." Tarra turned. It was Pamela, of course, as she had known it would be, with glowing face and dazzling smile aimed at Kaynon. "How wonderful to see you again so soon."

"Hello, Pamela," Kaynon drawled, his free hand finding Tarra's elbow.

Pamela wore an outré outfit of electric-blue wrap

shorts, teamed with a white linen jacket that brushed her hips. Underneath the jacket was a Tahiti print halter suspended from a white rope tie. Her escort was evidently the man she had been talking to last night when Kaynon wasn't available, Steve Adams, a young man who was both an artist and a volunteer at the gallery. From behind Pamela, Dede, in a black and white sundress that bared her shoulders, held Vince Malone's hand and grinned at her.

"Hi, Tarra. If we'd known you were going to be here, we'd have made it a party."

"But we can, anyway," Pamela exclaimed, putting her hand on Kaynon's arm. "Do come and sit with us."

"Sorry." Kaynon was curt. "We're already set up at another table."

"Well, let's get together after we've all eaten," Pamela insisted. "We're going over to a small club in Geneseo to dance afterwards. Say you'll come with us." She turned those limpid eyes up to Kaynon and flashed her most persuasive smile.

"We'll talk about it," Kaynon said noncommittally. "Now, if you'll excuse us . . ."

Back at the table Tarra took a deep breath, as if she had been through a marathon. Kaynon seemed not to notice, and after they had taken a bite or two, he launched into a casual conversation, which continued during the meal. They touched on movies they had seen, cities they had visited. He told her about San Francisco, and she told him about getting lost in Savannah one night and ending up on a street that was broken up by dozens of grassy squares and driving endlessly around each one. Kaynon, she discovered, had done several stints of summer stock during his college years, and he talked about it wittily and well. He had insights into acting and the kind of people who were driven to a profession that was riddled equally with pitfalls and glories.

"I was lucky enough to work with Robert Preston one

summer," he told her. "He has to be the epitome of a professional actor. Lines learned, on time, takes direction without a whimper."

"Why didn't you stay with it? I'm sure you must have been very good."

"I found it . . . confining. I wanted a larger world to work in. Few people realize that a supposedly glamorous life in the theater consists of varying parts of drafty theaters, indifferent motels, and tasteless food." He gave her a sudden, disarming smile. "I would have been a pushover for that apple pie."

"I must ask Mother for her recipe," she said lightly.

His eyes caught and held hers. "I'll hold you to that." His glance flickered over her shoulder to the general direction of the larger table where Pamela, Dede, and their escorts sat. "Well—do you want to join the mob scene?"

She shrugged, not knowing what his feelings were. Perhaps he wanted to see Pamela, dance with her. "It's up to you."

"If it's up to me, we'll forget it."

She gave him a sober look. "Are you sure that's wise? You're going to be working with all those people, remember?"

"I already have been. I started two weeks ago—remember?" he echoed, teasing her. "Is Dede a friend of yours?"

Tarra nodded, thinking of the nights she had gone to stay with Dede when she could no longer tolerate being in the apartment alone, knowing Bryant was out with another woman. "Yes, she is."

"Will she be offended if we refuse to come along?"

"I doubt it, but I couldn't say for sure."

He shrugged. "I suppose an hour out of the evening won't kill us."

"If you'd rather not—"

He said softly, "Then, on the other hand, it will give me a chance to dance with you."

40

"Do you have trouble making decisions?" she said with a touch of mockery.

"Well, yes—and no."

She laughed. Only a man as secure as Kaynon could have joked about his decision-making ability.

"There's one decision I haven't had trouble making," he murmured while she was still smiling.

"What's that?" They had had wine with their dinner, and she leaned forward slightly to pick up her glass by its slender stem.

"Whether or not I want to make love to you."

The glass hung suspended in midair for a moment before she could finish moving it to her lips. The wine had an extra bite to its dry flavor. She set the glass down carefully.

"You promised," she said huskily.

"I'm not touching you," he told her. "I'm only talking love."

She took another sip of wine and wondered if it was wise to mix alcohol with the potency of this man. As she replaced the glass on the table, he said, "And you *are* listening, aren't you?"

"Would you mind if we—changed the subject?"

He leaned back in the chair, but she was very much aware of his eyes on her face. "Would you like some coffee?"

"Yes, please."

The waitress saw his signal at once, and after listening to his request, flashed a smile and hurried away.

She refrained from commenting on his ability to get excellent service and wondered if it was her imagination that Pamela's laughter seemed to rise to the level of her consciousness a trifle too often, sound a bit too strident. *Damn,* she told herself. *Don't be that way.*

But an hour later, when the six of them were crammed around a table at the drink-and-dance bar and Pamela had somehow managed to insert herself next to Kaynon on the other side from Tarra, she had difficulty hiding her annoyance. Women had pursued Bryant just as ruthlessly, and Pamela's behavior rang all kinds of bells, none of them pleasant.

The band, a group of young people in their early twenties, was playing a current Top Forty tune. The floor was three times the size of most dance floors, and several couples were already dancing, their reflections bouncing off the floor-to-ceiling mirror on one wall as they moved in rapid rhythm to the music. A young girl stood behind the wrought iron railing, watching with a wistful look on her face while several other couples sat around the room, drinks in front of them.

"The music is great, isn't it," Dede said and smiled at Vince.

He took his cue. "Would you like to dance?"

"Oh, yes," and they moved out on the floor.

The six of them had been seated at a table meant to accommodate four, and Kaynon lifted his arm to rest it on the back of Tarra's chair.

"Steve doesn't dance," Pamela said. Then to Tarra: "You'll loan Kaynon to me for just one dance, won't you?"

"Don't I have anything to say about this?" The mockery was there in Kaynon's voice, but whether it was directed at her, Pamela, or himself, she couldn't tell.

"You'll have to ask Kaynon," she said coolly. "He's hardly mine to *loan.*"

Pamela rose and tugged at his hand. "Please come and dance with me, Kaynon. I don't want to to sit out the whole evening."

Kaynon gave Tarra a bland look and got to his feet. "Keep her company, Steve," he said with a proprietorial air.

Steve straightened as if he had been given orders by an employer. "Yes, sir," he said deferentially, shifting his legs to allow Pamela to walk in front of him, reddening under

42

his tan. He was young, twenty-two, Tarra guessed, and no match for either Pamela or Kaynon.

She tried not to watch them dancing, but she couldn't keep her eyes off that masculine figure that moved to the rhythm of the music with a pantherish male grace. He didn't take Pamela into his arms; they stood a foot away from each other, only touching occasionally as he caught her hand to turn her around. The pulsing beat of the music and the ability to see herself as she moved seemed to act as a stimulus to Pamela to discard her inhibitions. She was also discarding her jacket. Tarra watched with disbelief as Pamela slowly and erotically moved first one shoulder out of her jacket and then the other. Kaynon's eyes seemed to be fastened on her. *Whose wouldn't be?*

Her feet moving to the throbbing beat of the music, Pamela danced closer to Kaynon and wrapped her arms around his waist. She had her jacket in her hands, and with undulating movements, still dancing, she tied the sleeves around his waist under his suit coat.

The dance floor was illuminated with a shifting light that made it impossible to see Kaynon's reaction. Pamela stood on the floor clad only in a halter and shorts and lifted her arms to place them on his shoulders while she threw her head back. It was a primitive and erotic action, and yet, somehow, such a pathetic bid for his attention.

A waiter passed their table, unknowingly cutting off her view of the dance floor. When he asked if they'd like their drinks freshened, Tarra nodded gratefully. Her headache of that morning returned in full force, and while she knew a drink wouldn't be an effective cure, she hoped it would dull the pain.

He returned with the drinks. She pushed aside Steve's protests and insisted on paying for them. While she was getting the money out of her purse, the music ended. By the time she had given the young man his money and lifted her head, Kaynon had rid himself of Pamela's jacket and

43

was escorting her back to the table. The tawny-haired woman carried her jacket in her hand.

She had tablets in her purse and thought she could take two surreptitiously in the confusion of Kaynon and Pamela's arrival at the table, but as he sat down, Kaynon caught the tilted action of her head and knew at once what she had done.

"Aren't you feeling well?"

"I have a slight headache, that's all. I'll get over it in a moment or two . . ."

"It's the damn smoke," he growled. "These places never have enough air. Come on. Let's get out of here."

"You're not leaving?" Pamela cried plaintively.

"We've had enough. Carry on, Steve."

"Yes, sir," he said again, and Tarra was beginning to wonder if he could say anything else or if he was that much in awe of Kaynon.

"Kaynon, don't go." Pamela caught his arm. "We were having such fun."

This time Tarra could see his face, and if she had been Pamela, she would have shriveled up into a little ball. He was smiling, but it was a pitying, placating gesture. "The lady I came with," the emphasis was obvious, "has a headache. I am taking her home."

Pamela scowled, and Steve moved in his chair, recrossing his legs. Kaynon looked at him. "Dance with her. It isn't difficult. Anyone can do it."

It was a harsh, two-edged sword he sliced with, and even Pamela reddened at its thrust. "He'll be just as good as you are," she said spitefully to Kaynon.

"I'm sure," Kaynon murmured dryly, and took Tarra's arm.

Outside, the night air was warm, but it was fresh and breathable and pleasant. He guided her to the car, and when they were inside, he said, "Why didn't you say something sooner about your head?"

"I couldn't very well drag you off the dance floor, could I?"

"You were the one who threw me to that female barracuda in the first place."

"How was I to know you felt that way about her?" she said, her own temper rising as she sat locked inside the intimate confines of the car with him, "last night you were kissing her."

"Yes—" he leaned closer, and unconsciously, she tensed, "because I wanted to make you jealous. I wanted to get under your skin. I wanted to make you as aware of me as I am of you . . ." He pulled her across the divided seat to press his mouth on hers.

It wasn't a kiss so much as it was a declaration—a declaration of his power over her. Yet his mouth didn't hurt or maim. Even in his anger he was considerate of her. And even in her anger he was getting to her. That warm mouth had the power to change her universe, rearrange the entire structure of her body to one great ache. She had lived without a man for a year and had not felt a thing, but now Kaynon's determined mouth and man's body made her feel as if she had been tossed headlong into a warm sea of desire.

All those subtle little adjustments that a man makes when he discovers the woman in his arms is responding, Kaynon made. His mouth softened, persuaded. His hands lost their need to restrain and instead spread delight down her back and over her hips in much the same way they had that afternoon. His tongue explored, teased, devastated. She allowed herself the luxury of doing what she had wanted to do all evening. She pressed her hand against the bareness of his throat and felt cold metal on warm, hair-crisp skin.

When her fingertips touched the hollow and began to rub it sensuously, he pulled away. "I thought you had a headache," he murmured and pressed his lips to her temple.

"The aspirins must be working," she said softly.

"They aren't the only thing that's working," he muttered, and with a reluctance that gave her a little pang of pleasure, he removed his arm from around her and started the car.

The trip back to the cottage seemed to be over far too soon—and yet not soon enough. For she knew when they pulled into the driveway, she had lost the will to say no. There would be nothing to prevent him from simply taking her by the arm and going with her into the cottage . . . and staying the night.

CHAPTER THREE

He did take her arm and guide her into the cottage, but once the lights were on and he glanced around as if to satisfy himself that no one lurked in the shadows, he turned to her—and she knew from the look on his face that he didn't intend to stay. She felt a strange mixture of relief and regret.

"You wanted time," he said coolly, and then, when her guard was down and she believed she was safe, he raised his hand and touched her, brushing his fingers down the deeply cut neckline of her dress to caress the side of her rounded, exposed curve. Before she had time to move away, he trailed his fingertips back up and favored her other breast with the same feather-light touch. "I'm enough of an artist to know that anticipation is half the fun," he murmured.

While she was still in shock, he leaned forward to press a kiss between her warm curves. His mouth lingered momentarily on her exposed skin, and the air drained from her lungs, and while she was struggling to keep him from feeling the trembling reaction of her body, the dark auburn head lifted. "Tarra. Your name doesn't fit you," he mocked gently, "you have no mercy at all." He stood looking at her for a long moment. A thousand things buzzed inside her head—protests, denials, coldly cutting words that would tell him in no uncertain terms to stay away.

But none of them came out of her mouth. She was on

a roller coaster, hurtling down the hill toward the reality that was Kaynon—and there was nothing to stop her.

As if he read her thoughts, he smiled, a slow, knowing smile. Then he turned, and the squeak of the screen door told her he had let himself out.

She had long ago fallen into the habit of sleeping late on Sunday mornings, but after her evening with Kaynon, her late sleep was interrupted with dreams, weird reality-based dreams with Kaynon weaving in and out of them like a specter. She woke up and looked at the clock, feeling lethargic, unrested. It was only ten, and she rolled over, determined to go back to sleep, when the phone by her bed rang.

"You sound lovely this morning," Dede's cheerful voice said over the wire. Then her tone changed, softened. "I'm not—interrupting anything, am I?"

"If you mean am I sleeping with Kaynon," she said dryly, "no. The only thing you're interrupting is my sleep."

"Oh, sorry. Bad night?"

"You might say that."

"Look, I'm calling to apologize for horning in on your act last night. I wouldn't have been with Pam at all, but the guys are friends and we just sort of got together yesterday afternoon and decided we wanted to drive down to the lake again. I could have died when I saw you out with Kaynon. And then when Pamela practically draped herself over him the minute she saw him in the restaurant—I wanted to sink right through the floor. It's a good thing Vince is as tolerant as he is."

"How are things going in that department?" Tarra asked, coming awake by degrees.

She could almost see Dede's white teeth flashing in a grin. "Slow. But progressing. If he's too poky, maybe I'll have to take a lesson from Pamela. Lord! Did you see her out on the dance floor?"

48

"Who didn't?"

"I hated to go back and sit down at the same table with her. Poor Steve. He tried so hard to play out his part, but after you and Kaynon left, all she did was drink and sulk. It was altogether a . . . different evening, I'll say that. Vince and I danced as much as we could, but I was glad when it was time to leave."

"Sounds like she managed to ruin everybody's evening."

There was a pause. Dede said, "Listen, I don't know whether I should say this or not, but—be careful, won't you?"

"I'm a big girl now," Tarra said dryly, and Dede laughed. "Oh, you thought I meant Kaynon. No, it's not him you should be wary of, although maybe you should, but that's your problem. Anyway, Pamela's the one to watch out for. She's a prize bitch, to put it mildly. I've seen her be vindictive when she wants her way. And she obviously wants Kaynon."

Dede rattled on, telling her about Vince, but Tarra found it difficult to concentrate. As if she could sense Tarra's attention wandering, Dede said suddenly, "Well, I suppose I'd better let you go and let you get back to your rusticating. I don't know how you do it. I couldn't stand to live down there for one day, let alone fourteen. Don't you worry about leaving your lovely apartment and your art collection in the city that long?"

Tarra smiled. "My collection doesn't run my life. Besides, Dad installed an alarm system for me."

"To each his own, I guess. Of course, I suppose life on the lake will be a lot more interesting with Kaynon Edwards living next door. For him, I might even be tempted to go 'country.' "

"You're hopeless," Tarra said, laughing, and found that by the time Dede concluded the conversation and said good-bye, she felt infinitely better, except that . . . she sank back into the pillow, Dede's warning buzzing around in her head. Was Dede correct in her assumption that Pamela carried her obsessive envy to a point just short of criminality? She tried to remember how long the woman had been Eric's secretary. Two years? Three?

Later she was still thinking about Pamela and feeling that vague sense of unease when she stood in the kitchen filling the teakettle. She was so engrossed in her thoughts that when the phone rang again, she nearly dropped the little green pot. Carefully, she set the kettle down on the stove and picked up the receiver of the wall phone, nerves prickling under her skin. She couldn't think of anyone who might be calling her except—

"Hello, darling. How are you?"

The feminine voice was not the one she had expected to hear. "Mother? Where are you? You sound as if you're next door."

Her mother laughed. "We're in Switzerland, and the reason you can hear me so well is because of satellites and microwaves and I don't know what all lovely scientific advances. They assured me before I called that I'd have a better connection from here than I would if I were in the United States where everything's still cable. The weather's beautiful. We sent you a card saying 'wish you were here.' "

"Thanks," Tarra said dryly. "Having a good trip?"

"An absolutely wonderful trip. Wait until you see the things I've managed to buy for your Oriental collection. Some of the most darling little netsuke—with heads and eyes that move."

Her mother knew that the little decorative carved toggles that secured the ancient Japanese man's pouch to his belt were a favorite of Tarra's. She hesitated, the old specter of Bryant still hovering. How long did it take to convince your mind you really were free? "I hope you didn't pay an outrageous price for them."

"Now would I do that?" Her mother's voice had a wounded sound, but she did tend to get carried away, and her ideas of the value were not always supported by facts. If she liked something, she bought it.

"Wait till you see the *pièce de résistance*. It's for you, of course." Her mother paused, and Tarra knew what she was thinking. She was remembering Bryant, too. Before Tarra could protest, her mother enthused, "A choir of lovely Oriental girls in terra-cotta—complete with the music director herself in an outrageous pointed apron."

Tarra's indrawn breath betrayed her. "Are you serious?"

Her mother rushed on, leaving the important words unsaid. "Wasn't it a find? It was in the most unlikely-looking shop in London. I can't wait to have you see it. It is yours, of course; I bought it for you. How is the weather there?"

"Beautiful. Hot and sunshiny. When are you coming home?"

"Two weeks from Friday." There was a little pause, and then her mother said lightly, "Enjoying your vacation?"

"Yes, very much. No rushing around," Tarra said carefully. "Just lots of reading and swimming and catching some sun's rays." An unruly memory rose of the warmth of a man's hand on her back.

"Well, take care of yourself, darling, and don't swim out too far alone. Promise me you won't."

She smiled. "I promise not to drown myself."

"Good, I'm glad to hear it." Tarra's matter-of-fact words made that vaguely worried tone leave her mother's voice. They both knew her mother wasn't worried about her drowning. She had been afraid Tarra might brood. "I'd let you talk to your father, but he went out to get some filters for his pipe. He can call you next week." Her mother, once she had said what she wanted to say, was anxious to complete the call.

"I'll look forward to it."

She cradled the phone, feeling that familiar little excitement mingled with guilt. She could almost tell from the

51

feeling in her bones that the figures her mother had found were old, valuable, and authentic. Marion Hallworth had an uncanny sense of what was real and what was fake and an almost intuitive way of finding valuable ceramics in out-of-the way places.

She turned away from the phone and stared out the window at the lake, those old emotions still churning inside her. She shook herself mentally. She was free now. She had a perfect right to feel happy about her mother's purchase. But habits die hard. Two years ago she wouldn't have been happy. Two years ago she would have worried about Bryant's scathing comments.

"You have a fine, logical mind, darling," he had said. "Why do you clutter it up with that antique garbage?"

She had dug in her heels. "It's not garbage."

He shook his head and looked at her as if she were not quite bright. "Preoccupation with the past is for people whose lives are so empty they aren't interested in the present."

"That's not true," she had shot back. "My parents' lives are not empty."

"Aren't they?" he had sneered. "Your parents spend a hell of a lot of time worrying about you."

"Perhaps with good cause," she had returned angrily, wishing her voice were not marred by the husky trembling. "You're not very secretive about your . . . dissatisfaction with me. They . . . see you out with your . . . alternative amusements."

It had been the beginning of the end. And now she was totally immune to Bryant—which was a good thing, since they still worked in the same law office. The day she met him in the hall with a gorgeous girl with long blond hair she had felt nothing, absolutely nothing. But it was awkward. She had looked forward to this vacation, for the chance to relax away from those occasional encounters with him.

A rueful smile curved her mouth. He had been astound-

52

ed when she told him she was not going to look for another job. "It doesn't bother me to see you occasionally," she said, watching his mouth drop with pleasure. "If it bothers you—go somewhere else. I'm staying here."

His face had reddened with anger. She might have felt better if their quarrel had been only between themselves. She could have taken almost anything from Bryant, she thought, if he hadn't attacked her parents and her friends. But he had. He had begun to see other women within a matter of months after their marriage, and he had somehow turned everything around, made her the scapegoat, accused her of being so tied to her art collection, so wrapped up in her parents that she left no room in her life for him. That she was still a child, who didn't know what it meant to be a wife, to be a woman. It had taken Tarra some time to realize how flimsy an excuse for his infidelity he had chosen. For no matter how much time she made for Bryant in her life, no matter how much attention she lavished upon him, it was never quite enough. It was his scathing comments about her parents that stung her almost as deeply as his unfaithfulness, both compelling her to end the marriage quickly.

Tarra looked soft and feminine with her long brown hair and her warm brown eyes, but she had a stubborn streak a mile wide and an unyielding sense of loyalty. Theodore Hallworth was a surgeon and as busy as most, yet he always had time for her. He was enthusiastic about art—and he wanted to share that part of his life with her. She remembered tagging around in museums with him when she was hardly old enough to know what he was talking about. "Look at this, Tarra," he'd say. "Look at the way the artist has just suggested the sway of the tree in the wind with one long stroke of the brush." Or, "Feel this, honey. Feel where the sculptor shaped the marble to resemble the curve of a man's muscle."

It was her father who first introduced her to Oriental pottery. He had given her her first Ming vase, her first

T'ang horse. He had bought them years ago, at reasonable prices, before the craze for Oriental art made prices soar. Now she had to limit her acquisitions to one or two a year.

She hoped her mother hadn't paid a fantastic price for the musicians. She pushed the unwelcome thoughts of Bryant out of her mind and went upstairs to change into her suit. Out in the lake, she could wash away the thoughts of him.

After she had swum for almost an hour, she got out of the water. She had seen nothing of Kaynon. He had not emerged from his cottage, though she could see the car parked in his driveway. She was curious, wondering why he hadn't come out for a dip. Inwardly she shrugged. She wasn't going to go over. She wasn't Pamela.

It was almost dark when the knock came at her door. It was Kaynon, and he was scowling. "Do you have any candles?"

He was dressed to the nines again, in a shimmering silk shirt that was either silver or gray, she wasn't sure which. Surprisingly enough, he wore a tie, a narrow black one caught with a silver clip that resembled a satyr with a lute. His black trousers clung to his muscular thighs.

"What . . . kind of candles?"

"Tall ones—for a dinner table. I'm entertaining a client here for dinner tonight. I gave Eric a list of things I needed, and he either forgot or hid them so well I can't find them. The caterer called up, her driver is sick and I've got to go into Avon to pick up the food, which is a good hour wasted, and by the time Lucille does get here, I'll be in no mood to talk to her."

"Lucille? Not . . . Lucille Stratton-Duncan."

His eyes narrowed. "Yes, that's her. Do you know her?"

"Only by reputation." She hesitated and then said softly, "Lucy in the Sky with Diamonds."

"What?"

"It's an old Beatle tune, and Mrs. Stratton-Duncan has the right initials."

Kaynon leaned back against the door. "So she does. Is that an in joke in the city?"

Tarra shrugged. "I suppose so. I heard it years ago, that and the fact that she only wears colors that start with *b* —black, brown, beige, and blue." She turned and went into the dining room. "I think Mother keeps some down here for the occasional thunderstorm. Let me look."

She opened the middle drawer, the one that didn't stick as much as the others. "You're in luck." She brought out two white tapers wrapped in crinkly transparent paper. "They haven't even been used. Mrs. Stratton-Duncan will be suitably impressed."

He had followed her and now was leaning against the arched door that led into the dining room. "I get the feeling you don't approve."

"It isn't my place to approve or disapprove. The way you make your living has nothing to do with me." She held out the candles. "As I said," she let her eyes roam over his well-groomed masculine body, "I'm sure Mrs. Stratton-Duncan will be suitably impressed."

Dark red color moved under his cheekbones. "You've come out into the deep end with a vengeance, haven't you?" He reached out and instead of taking the candles, caught the hand that held them in a grip that made her wince. "Well, let me tell you something, lady. You're in over your head. You've swallowed the malicious stuff the press and my brother say about me whole without the slightest qualm, haven't you? My God, I hope you choke on it." He drew her closer, and she twisted her arm, trying to get free. His eyes burned with anger. "I'd forgotten how supposedly intelligent people like you accept that trash as truth without a second thought just because it's in print." His grip tightened, and she nearly cried out with pain. "You didn't really want more time, did you? You just didn't want to sully yourself with a man of my reputation. A few kisses are all right, but anything more—forget it."

He jerked her closer and caught her between the hard

surface of the buffet and the even harder surface of his muscular thighs. He was furious, his body tense and coiled, like a snake ready to strike.

She was powerless to move against the strength of his hold and paralyzed by the knowledge that he was at least partially right.

"Kaynon, I—" but being close to him seemed to rob her of speech.

And he didn't want to hear what she had to say. "No," he muttered, lowering his head. "You believe what you've heard—why should I be the one to disillusion you?"

There was a subtle male domination in the way he took her mouth, a need to subdue. But there was tenderness, too, and a warm, sensual understanding of her that melted her resistance before it surfaced. She still had the candles in her hand, but Kaynon didn't seem to mind as her hands went around his back. She was the one who regretted not being able to place both her palms on the silvery texture of his shirt and feel the warmth of the man beneath.

Kaynon had nothing in his hands but her, and he let them wander over her hips and back, one hand moving under the brief T-shirt she wore, to explore the hollow of her back that was exquisitely sensitive to his touch, the other cupping her nape, tilting her head back to allow him to deepen the kiss as he probed with his tongue. The insidious need to move closer, to have more of him, was beginning; she could feel it moving up through her.

With her free hand she caressed his nape and melted against him, inviting him to drink his fill of her mouth. When he lifted his lips, she moaned softly and pressed her mouth against the firm outline of his chin, brushed the smoothly shaven cheeks, and continued over his skin to the tip of his ear. He smelled clean and fragrant with the scent of after-shave and cologne, and the scent was going directly to her brain like a potent aphrodisiac. When she took his earlobe gently between her teeth and tugged at it, he shuddered in response—and dropped his hands from her body. Instantly he moved away.

"Now," he said. "Shall we talk about *your* integrity? Because every time I hold you, you invite me to make love to you." He paused and then said heavily, "And you know what kind of man I am."

She faced him and gathered her courage. "I only know what happens when you touch me. And I can't—change that." She didn't add that she wouldn't even if she could.

Her honest answer seemed to mollify him somewhat. "None of the stories are true."

"Then why don't you—deny them?"

He arched an eyebrow. "There are things that are too damn precious to give away at any price, and my freedom is one of them. I won't rearrange my life to suit my father or my brother or the press."

"You're very lucky. Lots of people aren't so fortunate," she said coolly, hurting, knowing that he was warning her he wouldn't be trapped into a permanent commitment with a woman.

"I've worked for my freedom," he said through gritted teeth. "I declared my independence from my father and his money when I was eighteen, and I've never looked back."

"Congratulations," she said coolly, thrusting the candles at him. "Why don't we light one of these in your honor?"

"You don't believe me, do you?"

"Why should I?" she cried, forgetting that she had no right to question him, knowing only that she had admitted how much his touch affected her and he had responded by declaring his independence. "Do you think I'm so stupid I don't realize why you're entertaining her here instead of taking her out?" When she realized what she had said, what she was implying, she could have bitten off her tongue.

He wasn't pleased, either. His eyes blazed, and for a

moment she thought he would hit her. Then he ran a hand through his hair in an exasperated gesture. "I don't know why I'm explaining it to you—or why I should give a damn what you think about me—but as it happens, the lady has a phobia about eating in public. You already mentioned her clothes fetish. Well, she's a kook in other ways, too. I've had a devil of a time arranging this interview. And now everything's shot to hell."

The gesture and the words made him look so much like her father after a harried day in the office that suddenly she believed him. He was working—working at what he did best.

Abruptly she said, "I'll go to Avon and pick up the food for you if that would help."

He gazed at her, his face stark. A silence seemed to pulse through the cottage, heavy with things unspoken. Then he said huskily, "Yes. Yes, it would. That way I won't run the risk of having her come to an empty cottage while I'm gone."

He stuck his hand in his pocket, brought out some bills, and gave them to her. "The stuff is in my name at that seafood place on Highway Fifteen. I'm not sure how much it will be. There should be enough here to pay for the food and put some gas in your car while you're there."

"I have a full tank," she said easily and handed him the candles.

He took them this time, and his shoulders moved in a careless, dismissive movement. "Suit yourself."

When he was gone, she picked up her purse and went out to the car. All the way down the winding lake road she thought about what she had said, how badly she had misjudged him, and how furious he was with her. If he felt that strongly about being maligned, why didn't he fight back? Why didn't he let the public know that he was a dedicated fund raiser and nothing else? She tried to think back on just exactly what she had read about Kaynon and where it was said, but she couldn't remember a thing.

Most of her information had come from Eric. With a little shock she realized how prejudiced that information might be. It didn't take a genius to see that he was jealous of Kaynon. Kaynon was a man any man might envy, let alone one whose activities were restricted by a damaged heart.

The smell of seafood—shrimp, haddock, and clams—mingled and tantalized her nose as she walked into Jomo's Seafood Shop. Luckily, Kaynon's order was ready and waiting for her in steaming white cartons. She paid the man, who looked as if he sampled his own food too frequently, and let him help her carry it out to her car. He showed her how to stack the cartons on the backseat so that they wouldn't slide off.

When she had driven back to the cottage and was climbing the stairs up to the patio, Kaynon heard her and came out, swinging the door open for her. "You should have let me bring it in. Just set everything in on the counter. I'll take it from there."

Through the door of the kitchen she caught a glimpse of the dining room. The chandelier was softly lit, and under it, the table was spread with white linen and gleaming silver. The candles stood in carved teak holders, and between them delicate purple wild flowers floated in a low bowl.

"You improvise well," she said, finding him watching her.

He opened his mouth as if he were going to say something and then closed it. She had a sudden intuitive perception of what he was going to say, and she felt a wave of sadness sweep over her. He no longer cared about bantering in a light, sexual vein with her. Those days were over.

"Thank you, Tarra," he said formally, and she inclined her head just as formally.

"No problem. Good luck tonight." She turned and went

out the door and clattered down the steps before he could answer.

At home in the suddenly quiet and confining living room, she buried herself in her historical romance. By a supreme effort of will she kept reading, even though by now she was enough into the book to realize that the hero had hair the exact same shade as Kaynon's and his same fierce love for independence.

She turned on some music, determined not to be aware of the hour that Mrs. Stratton-Duncan's car left Kaynon's cottage. She succeeded, at least partially, because when she went to bed, the half-mile-long white Cadillac was gone and she hadn't heard it pass by.

She spent a restless night, and when she did finally doze off toward early morning, she slept only a few hours. The sound of Kaynon's car leaving woke her around six o'clock, and from then on, sleep was impossible. Instead, she lay there, just thinking.

She got through the day somehow, but as the sun went down and turned the lake a delicious pink color, she was far too conscious of the fact that Kaynon's car had not returned to its usual spot.

He didn't return from the city that night or all the next day and night. She supposed he had been working late and stayed in town at his father's place. Wednesday afternoon, around five o'clock, when the sky was filled with clouds and it looked as if rain would make it impossible to swim or sun, she was strongly considering going back into the city herself to look for more reading material and do some laundry, when she heard the sound of his car crunching over the gravel.

The car door slammed, followed by a boom of thunder. Rain came up quickly on the lake, sometimes accompanied by sharp and tearing gusts of wind. The sound of the thunder echoed in the surrounding hills with more rolling booms than anywhere else she had ever experienced a storm, and of course, the water was an attraction for lightning.

She told herself it was the rain and the sudden darkness rather than Kaynon's arrival that made her decide to postpone her trip to the city, and went to look for a flashlight. The power invariably failed during an electrical storm; they had come to count on it, and that was one of the reasons she had been able to provide Kaynon with candles. Her mother always kept them on hand for just such an emergency.

She looked in the kitchen cupboard, the upstairs closet, the shelf under the stairs. She couldn't find the flashlight. She went out into the kitchen, deciding she would fix herself a sandwich now in case the electricity did go out and she had to stumble around in the dark. The lightning cracked, and thunder followed almost immediately, telling her the strike was close—and the lights flickered and went out.

She cursed softly and wished she had been a little quicker. The rain started, coming across the lake in a great gray sheet, and she remembered she had left her upstairs bedroom window open. She dashed up and closed it, and as she came down the stairs, she heard the pounding on the door merging with the thunder. She flew to the kitchen, knowing that whoever was out there had to be getting soaked.

"Kaynon!"

She opened the door wide, and he swept in on a gust of cold wind and rain, his light silk shirt speckled with drops of moisture. He looked haggard, as if he hadn't slept a minute in the two days since she had last seen him, and his hair was mussed and flat with wetness. In his hand were the two candles she had lent him.

"You came out in the rain with those?" She was incredulous. "You shouldn't have. You're soaked."

"Does the power always go off the minute there's a few drops of rain?"

61

"Usually," she said matter-of-factly, handing him a towel. "Here. Dry your hair."

He shook his head. "No, thanks. It will just get wet when I go back out anyway." He hunched his shoulders as if he were stiff and sore. "I thought I was going to come home and have a nice hot bath and relax. God. Will nothing go right?"

She leaned back against the counter and wrapped the towel over her arm. "Bad day?"

"No," he said, his voice heavy with irony. "It's been a terrific day. I love to argue with my brother and my father. It's my idea of a relaxing afternoon."

She turned away and went into the dining room to get out the candleholders. She found a matchbook and it was limp with dampness, but at last she got a match to ignite. She carried the lighted candles back into the kitchen and set them down on the counter. He hadn't moved. She gathered up every scrap of her courage and said casually, "Why don't you stay here until the storm lets up? They don't usually last too long."

"No, thanks," he said curtly, wounding her. "I'll go in a minute. I just need to get my breath back."

But he wasn't breathing heavily, and he didn't seem to be under a physical strain. There was something else, though, something very unlike his usual cool self-control percolating through his body, and in the flickering candlelight, Tarra saw the tautness around his mouth, the glaze in his eyes.

He said coldly, "If I'd known thunderstorms that wake the dead were common down here, I'd never have moved in."

"Kaynon." She swallowed and moved closer to him. He smelled of wet leaves and rain and cigarette smoke. "You aren't . . . afraid, are you?"

He didn't answer.

She moved closer, scarcely daring to breathe. "Are you?"

He began to talk, and it was as if he had gone somewhere else, leaving only the dead sound of his voice. "Once, when I was in summer stock in New England, I was out playing golf on a rare afternoon off with a good friend of mine. The storm came up almost out of nowhere. We were hiking toward the clubhouse, laughing about making sure we told the truth about our scores, when the lightning hit him. He couldn't have been more than four feet away from me."

"Kaynon." She touched his arm. "I'm sorry."

"He died before they got him into the ambulance. I've hated the damn sound of thunder ever since."

A loud crack echoed through the sky, and he tensed. She put her arms around his stiff, unyielding body. "I'll hold you," she whispered. "Let me."

He was still for a moment, and then he caught her arms and thrust her away. "I don't need your pity—I don't want it." He whirled around and yanked the door open and was gone, walking through the rain and the wind and the thunder that he hated rather than take the comfort that she offered him.

As she had known it would, the storm abated within the hour. The power was restored shortly after that. But the storm within her raged on. She paced restlessly back and forth like a fettered lioness. She had been handed a monumental problem, and she simply couldn't come up with a solution. She didn't want to be Kaynon's enemy. She wanted to take back the awful things she had said to him. She wanted to tell him that she believed in him . . . and she wanted to comfort him because he had had a miserable day and at the end of it he had been reminded about the good friend he had lost.

But she couldn't. Because he would never forgive her. She had made her opinion of him all too clear, and now he wanted nothing to do with her. She circled around once again, kicking a book out of her way. She had no weapons in her armory, no idea of how to go about regaining his interest. She couldn't just go up to him and say *I'm sorry for what I thought, what I believed. I don't believe it now. Let me into your life again. I don't like being your enemy . . .*

She was so engrossed in her pacing she hardly heard the knock on the door until it came the second time, louder. She stopped, her heart thudding. Composing herself, running her hands down the seam of her denim pants to rid them of the sudden film of perspiration, she walked to the door.

"You're going to wear out the carpet," he said without preamble as he stepped inside.

She realized then that she hadn't pulled the shades because of the storm. But her old defensiveness made her say, "What do you want?"

"You invited me to stay with you a few minutes ago." He had changed into denims and a blue button-down-the-front shirt, but on him the casual cut of denim and cotton was sensational. His mouth tilted in a slow smile that demoralized her. "I decided to take a rain check."

She said, "That's a terrible joke." He was inside the house because he had stepped in, but she made no move to invite him to stay. His mood was definitely mellower, but somehow, faced with the subject of her agonized thoughts, she couldn't seem to unbend.

"Before you decide I'm the original first-class heel, let me say that I've come over to apologize—something that I've never done to anyone before."

"All right," she said coolly, cutting him off because she was reluctant to have him humble himself any further, "apology accepted."

He seemed surprised by her abrupt acceptance, but he said no more. He made no move to go, either. In the rather pointed silence that followed, he glanced casually at the stove and saw the green teakettle. "Doesn't a once-in-a-lifetime apology rate a cup of coffee at least?"

She met his eyes and saw nothing there but a faint amusement. What a fool she was! She had been pacing the floor a minute ago, wishing for a chance to sweep away the animosity between them. Now she was being given the chance—and she was making a mess of it. "Yes, of course." She moved then, taking the kettle and holding it under the faucet. Her back was to him, but she was no less aware of his presence. When she turned around to place the kettle on the stove, she said, "Would you like to go into the living room and sit down?"

The stiff formality of the invitation made his eyes glitter for a moment. She pivoted to lead the way, and his expression was lost to her.

She indicated the sofa in front of the stone fireplace, but he took a pillow from one corner and bent his long legs to sit on the floor and stretch them out in front of him, his back against the front of the sofa. Glad that it was long, flowered, and curving, she sat in the far corner of it at a safe distance, knowing she wasn't going to be able to think of a thing to say. She needn't have worried. He laid his head back and closed his eyes.

She wasn't sure just how long he stayed like that, but it must have been several minutes because just when she was sure he was asleep, the lid rattled on the teakettle, telling her that the water was boiling. As she moved to get up, his voice stopped her. "Do you happen to have any tea in the house?"

"Would you prefer that to coffee?"

"Yes, if you don't mind."

Out in the kitchen she found the china flowered pot she used and wrapped the strings of three bags around the handle. She put the cups and the pot on the tray, along with the sugar and cream and slices of lemon.

He opened his eyes as she returned to the room and set the tray on the low table in front of him. She was forced to sit closer to him on the sofa in order to pour from the pot and hand him a cup.

"The Japanese have a whole ceremony for drinking tea. Did you know that?" he said in weary facsimile of his normal vital tones.

She knew it very well. "Yes, I've—heard of it."

His fatigue had made him less than alert or he surely would have questioned her about her knowledge. "It evolved out of Zen Buddhism and the desire to enjoy elegance and simplicity in the act of taking tea." He picked up his cup and went on, almost as if he were talking to himself. His words seemed therapeutic, and she did not feel the necessity of stopping him to explain that she was familiar with the ceremony.

"Everything has order—the way the host greets the guests, the way the guests admire the touch of beauty, a scroll or flower arrangement called an *ikebana,* the way the host stirs and pours the tea, the way the guests compliment him on it. All of which makes it sound as if there's a lot going on—which there isn't. The ceremony takes four hours if done right, and there is silence for most of that time so that all may enjoy a harmony of spirit and tranquillity of mind."

It gave her a strange feeling to hear him describe the ceremony which had always fascinated her. They shared so many interests. She opened her mouth to tell him so, when he said, "I wonder why only the Eastern civilizations seem to know the value of quiet? In the Western world we think we can assail our ears with constant noise and not have it bother us. That's one reason I drove forty miles tonight. I wanted to be where it was quiet." He looked at her. "And then to have that damn thunderstorm crashing over my head . . . I should never have come over here. I was in a foul mood."

"I did notice," she said lightly.

"But I still couldn't keep away," he said. "I hadn't seen you for two days, and I was hungry for the sight of you."

His words sent a stinging thread of excitement through her. Deliberately, he set his cup down on the table. "I've gone about as far as my male pride and my inhibitions will let me, Tarra." His gaze was steady under the dark red lashes. "The next move is up to you."

It was there again, that wry acceptance of himself, mingled with the vulnerability, the tenderness. He was asking her for some sign that she understood—and forgave him.

The silence continued, and when she made no move toward him, his lashes flickered down, as if he needed to hide the sight of his pain from her.

Driven by the thought that she had hurt him again, she made the monumental decision that would expose her to his rejection and scorn if he didn't want her.

She copied his own deliberate movements and set her cup down on the table. For a moment longer she sat, her heart pounding, but something stronger than fear was directing her. She rose and walked around the table, around his long legs. She sat down on the other side, away from the little table, facing him, her legs crossed under her, the curve of the couch forcing her close to his thigh. A little flame lit in his eyes, but he didn't move. He merely watched her—and waited. She avoided meeting his gaze, because she knew if she did and caught the slightest hint of derision in those jade-green depths, her courage would fail her. She lifted her hands to his shirt, slipping the first button he had fastened out of its hole. Her fingernails raked over his hair-crisp skin as she undid the next one.

"This isn't a standard part of the tea ceremony," he said huskily.

"Do you want me to stop?" She was serious, afraid of what his answer might be.

"I'm not sure." Amusement lurked in his voice. "I have trouble making decisions, remember?" She pulled away from him, but he caught her fingers in his warm hand and put them back on his chest. "You'd better keep on until I decide."

Relief made her giddy. The feeling of his warm skin under her hands was a heady pleasure. She said huskily,

67

marveling at her temerity, "I don't think I've ever seduced a man before. There should be rules, like there are for the tea ceremony. Tell me if I'm doing something wrong." She had reached the last button and was tugging his shirt away from the waistband of his pants.

"You may lack a little in subtlety, but it doesn't make your approach any less exciting." His hands were braced on the floor, as if he needed to lock them there to keep from touching her. His eyes never left her face. "Didn't you ever seduce your husband?"

"No."

"Why not?"

She gave him a long, steady look. "He made love to other women . . . and I couldn't—couldn't accept that. It—turned me off."

"I can see how it might."

She pressed her lips to the soft hollow of his throat and then let her mouth wander lower.

"My God." He lifted his hands and reached for her and in one swift movement, pulled her across his thighs and nestled her into his lap. "The man was an idiotic fool . . ."

He looked at her for a long, expressive moment, and she returned his look, wondering if he could read the surrender in her eyes. Perhaps he could, for he groaned softly and lowered his head.

CHAPTER FOUR

He kissed her warmly, possessively. The solid wall of his chest, bare because she had unbuttoned his shirt and pushed it aside, nudged against her arm. She moved slightly in order to slip her arm around behind him and wrap her hand around his waist. Her closer proximity forced her breasts against his chest. She was clutching him, clinging to him as if he were the one thing that would keep her afloat in this fast-rising tide that threatened to drown her. Just as she felt he would kiss the breath out of her, he raised his head. With a hand that was so gentle it made her heart leap, he brushed the strand of coffee-colored hair away from her cheek. "Brown eyes," he said softly. She buried her mouth against his neck under the curve of his jaw and feathered kisses down to the hollow of his throat. He made a low, almost tortured sound. "Do you know what you are doing to me?"

"Yes," she murmured, lifting her head, searching for a way to deny the desire her hands and mouth were revealing. "I'm helping you forget the pain."

He tensed. "You feel sorry for me—"

"Yes," she whispered, thinking she felt sorrier for herself. His attraction was getting to her. He was under her skin.

She moved toward him again, but he pushed her away. "Keep your sympathy," he said roughly.

His change of mood threw her. "What?"

"I said, keep your damn sympathy. I don't want it."

His face was hard and dark, and she half expected him to dump her out of his lap, but he didn't. And while she was trying to decide if she should explain, the phone rang.

She stared at him. His face was unreadable, his eyes shadowed by lashes. "Aren't you going to answer it?" The cool green eyes examined her impersonally.

He had shut her out, completely. She scrambled off his lap and went out into the kitchen, her mind blank. He was like a cave with hidden chasms that fell away to the center of the earth, and she kept falling into them.

Bruce Edwards's voice boomed in her ear. "Tarra. How are you, sweetheart? Look out and see if Kaynon's car is next door, would you? He left the city hours ago, but I can't get him to answer the phone. If he isn't in the bathtub or asleep, he must have had car trouble—or an accident."

"He's . . . here."

There was a sudden little silence while he absorbed that. Then, a droll, "Is he, indeed? Well, put him on, would you?"

He had followed her out to the kitchen, and he hadn't bothered to button up his shirt.

"It's your father," she said, holding out the receiver to him.

She went into the living room and put the cups back on the tray. When she returned to the kitchen, both sides of the conversation were easily audible to her. Bruce Edwards was talking at top speed and volume.

". . . we'll manage the parking problem somehow. Eric has agreed to suspend the admission fee for that day and include a story about Kaleidoscope in his monthly news release. As long as you agree to do all the liaison work with the Women's League and guarantee their cooperation, Eric has given his okay."

"Big of him," Kaynon murmured.

"You'll contact Hallmark and set a date for the latter part of August, then?"

"I'll contact them, but I don't know if we'll have a choice on the date."

His father was brusque. "Well, do the best you can. I'll talk to you tomorrow, but I thought I ought to call you and tell you about Eric's agreeing to your proposal. You looked pretty ragged when you walked out of here."

"Yeah. Thanks, Dad."

There was a silence. "Oh, Kaynon. Give my love to Tarra, will you?"

She heard the click of the receiver. Bruce Edwards was not a man to give his opponent a chance of rebuttal.

Kaynon replaced the receiver and turned. His eyes were shadowed with dark lashes, his hair mussed where she had touched it. "My father sends his love."

"I'll thank him the next time I see him," she said in a strained tone, feeling an unreasonable urge to hold her breath. When he made a move as if to go, she said quickly, "You've . . . resolved your argument with him?"

"Yes," he said. He hesitated and then added, "I wanted the gallery to sponsor a visit by Kaleidoscope. It's a traveling creative art laboratory that Hallmark has created for kids. Eric was dead set against it. But I suppose after I left the scene, my father talked reason—and money—to him. Eric can be approached through the practical side of things—a fact I forgot when I lost my temper with him this afternoon."

"He has to have money to pay staff and utility bills."

"Yes, thank God. Otherwise, I have a feeling, he'd put everything in a time capsule and say 'You may look at this art, for one day only, in the year 3000.'"

She had to smile at that. "You're exaggerating."

"Not much." He looked at her then. "Thanks for the tea."

"You're welcome."

He continued to look at her for another long moment, the expression on his face unreadable. She made a desperate attempt to keep her face as cool as his own. She dared

71

not reveal what she was thinking, that she wanted him to take her in his arms and press his mouth against hers. She wanted him to take her away—beyond thought and reason, beyond the need to make a choice. His expression darkened and his body tensed, and she knew he was going to go. Disappointment and unfulfilled longing seethed through her. She forced herself to stillness. He turned away, his unbuttoned shirt flaring out around his lean hips, bringing an ache to her throat for what might have been. The screen door squeaked as he let himself out, and she stood there, feeling alone and empty. She didn't understand him. He had been quite frank about wanting to make love to her, and yet, when she had given him the opportunity, he had rejected it because he believed she was motivated by sympathy. He was a complex man who lived life on his own terms and no one else's. There was no future in a relationship with him. She had to forget him.

The next day she found the conclusion far easier to arrive at than carry out. She relived the scene with him endlessly, wishing she had not felt the need to protect herself, wishing she had told him how much she wanted him, wishing she had ignored the phone and wrapped her arms around him and invited him to stay the night with her.

Around noon her relentless thoughts drove her to pack her laundry into the car and drive back to the city. A change of scene might remove Kaynon Edwards from her churning thoughts.

When she let herself into her apartment, she saw that everything was as she had left it, although the alcove looked empty without its *ikebana*. After her divorce she had moved into an older home close to Highland Park that had been converted to a fourplex. The high ceilings, wood floors, and good oak woodwork had attracted her from the first and were just the background she needed for her simple and elegant Oriental accessories. Whenever she was away, she seemed to see everything with new eyes and appreciate its beauty all over again, the Oriental carpet on the bare wood floor, the simple beige couch, the intricately painted Oriental panels she had found in New York City and mounted on swing rods to cover the floor-to-ceiling windows. She had converted a bay window into a tiny alcove that would seat four around a low table—an alcove that was kept in readiness for the tea ceremony.

Her thoughts veered. She remembered a hand holding a cup, a lean, well-formed hand with blunt-shaped nails and dark auburn hairs sprinkled on the back, and a low, masculine voice talking about the Way of Tea. . . .

She carried the laundry into the kitchen and began to sort it. She worked the rest of the day, dusting and cleaning the apartment. She had not bothered to call anyone and tell them she was back in the city for the day, which was why she was greatly surprised when, around seven, the doorbell chimed.

Dede stood outside, still wearing her working clothes, a sleek olive-green wrap dress and smooth-fitting black sandals. She was clutching a brown paper bag and the strap of her leather purse, and making a face as a strand of her short red hair blew across her mouth. She managed to brush it away with a free hand and said, "Hi. I saw your car. What are you doing back in the city? I brought dinner. Have you eaten?"

"Washing and no. Come on in."

Dede breezed through to the kitchen. "I brought spaghetti and sauce and cheese and bakery bread. To hell with dieting."

"I know—you just want my misery for your company."

"You've got it. Where's that big saucepan?"

"In the cupboard by the stove. Make yourself at home," she said dryly, knowing she could tease without causing hard feelings.

"Thanks," Dede shot back.

She heard the aluminum kettle bang on the stove and

smiled. Dede was not a restrained woman, but Tarra loved her for her impetuous generosity. Dede flew to her side at the first hint of trouble.

"How are things going with the luscious Mr. Edwards?" Dede said when Tarra came out into the kitchen to watch her fly around like a madwoman, getting the water ready, shaping the ground steak into meatballs.

"Don't ask. I think I'll give him up—in the interest of preserving my sanity. Is that homemade sauce?"

Dede nodded. "Mother's. What seems to be the problem?"

Tarra tried a casual shrug. "Too many barriers. I keep crashing on hidden reefs. I guess I'll have to turn him over to Pamela. She's so wrapped up in herself she'd never notice."

Dede dumped a generous amount of spaghetti into the boiling water and turned to face Tarra, her lips curved in a rueful smile. "I have a feeling that handing Mr. Edwards off to anybody would be like asking a male lion to please find another cave. He might be inclined to object—in a way that would make you back off in a hurry."

"That's possible," she said lightly. Needing to change the subject, she picked the one topic Dede would be willing to discuss. "How's Vince?"

"Terrific. We're going to the reception together. But if you think that's going to distract me from asking you about Kaynon—"

"What reception?"

"The one being held for Mrs. L.S.D. It's all very hush-hush at this point, but Pamela was supposed to call and invite you this morning. I heard Eric giving her specific instructions. Didn't she?"

"I suppose I didn't hear the phone—"

Dede made a contemptuous sound. "Of course, and I'm Bo Derek. I wonder how she thought she'd get by with that? Do you think Kaynon will ask you?"

74

"Right now the only thing Kaynon Edwards would ask me to do is take a flying leap into Conesus Lake."

Dede turned from the stove and gave her a long, searching look from under red-gold lashes. "That wasn't the way it looked the other night."

"Things change. Can I turn the meatballs?" It was a standing joke between them that Tarra was a disaster in the kitchen. Without waiting for her friend's reply she picked up a fork and carefully pushed the frying meat around in the deep pan.

"And you're not going to tell me a thing."

"There's nothing to tell. I told you, he's a complicated man, and I don't understand him. I'm not even sure I want to try."

Dede stirred the spaghetti, watching her. "It always throws you when the good-looking ones have brains, doesn't it? Somehow you expect them to be nothing but beautiful bodies running around in gyms and tennis courts."

Tarra said, "You're stereotyping."

"If I am, then it must be a stereotype that our gorgeous friend has come up against a time or two. You always hear about women that don't want to be thought of as just another pretty face, but what about men? Don't you suppose they get tired of being reminded how good-looking they are, too?"

She thought of Bryant. It never seemed to bother him. "What a horrible problem to have." Her tone was acerbic.

"Nobody wants to be taken at surface value," Dede said steadily. "Everybody wants people to look past the physical and see what a fine person they are underneath."

"I can't argue with that. I'm just not sure it applies to Kaynon."

The water bubbled in the pan and nearly came over the top. Dede grabbed a pot holder and snatched it away from the heat. "Of course it applies to him. Actually, I think there's a kind of—oh, I don't know—vulnerability about him. I think he's searching for something." She paused and gave a dramatic sigh. "I'd love to be that something," she looked at Tarra, "but you're much more his style."

"Did you intend to serve the spaghetti up in the same dish with the baloney?" she retorted.

"Yes," Dede shot back, laughing, "and poke them both down your throat at the same time."

"I might choke."

"I hope you do. It might bring you to your senses. You're so darn stubborn you can't see your nose in front of your face. You married Bryant and that was a mistake, so now you're afraid to trust your own feelings." Tarra opened her mouth to launch a counterattack, but Dede held up the long fork, a strand of spaghetti dangling from the end of it, her flag of surrender. "All right, all right. You win. I won't mention Kaynon Edwards again for the rest of my life—" she grinned impishly, "or at least until we've finished eating. Have you got any wine, or was I supposed to bring that too?"

She did have some wine. She brought it out of the refrigerator and poured it into the crystal glasses while Dede dished up the food.

Dede's casual conversation about Vince and the gallery carried them through the meal. By the time she had eaten the delicious food and drunk two glasses of the white wine, she was definitely feeling better.

"The reception is Saturday night. Will you stay in town for it or go back out to the lake?"

"Go back out, I guess. I hate to spend my vacation sitting here."

Dede hung up the towel and stood looking out into the living room. "I can think of worse places. But—to each his own. I've got to run. Listen, if you do decide to stay for the next couple of days, call me, will you? I hate to see you become a recluse during your vacation."

"Actually, I was planning on it. But I'll call you, I promise."

The apartment seemed empty when Dede left. She watered her plants, the jade and philodendron and African violets, and then changed her mind about leaving. She would stay in town for the weekend. There was no reason for her to go back to the lake. None at all.

She needn't have bothered rearranging her life to avoid him. Kaynon Edwards was out of town, Dede told her over the phone the next evening. He had gone to talk to the representatives of Kaleidoscope. She should have found that news a reason to relax, but instead she prowled the apartment, feeling like a tethered wildcat.

By the time Saturday night arrived and she went into the bedroom to dress for the reception, she was more than glad for an excuse to spend a long time getting ready. She stood under the shower too long, and then had to spend another fifteen minutes creaming into her skin the moisture the water had taken away. She had her entire wardrobe to choose from this time, and she decided to wear the apricot dress, a draped sheath that had a low V neckline, batwing sleeves, and a slit up the front that showed a glimpse of her elegant long legs. A wide belt in a creamy satin made her waist look wasp sized. With a slightly different hairstyle, one that bared one side of her face and let her coffee-colored mane fall forward on the other cheek, she looked cool and sophisticated.

She had no fear of running into Kaynon. He was still out of town, Dede had said. He was having trouble getting plane reservations, and he had called last night to warn his father that he didn't think he'd make it back in time for the reception. Eric had offered to be her escort, and she had accepted on an impulse. Now, as she transferred lipstick, comb, and tissues to the small silver purse she would need and heard the doorbell chime through the apartment, she regretted that impulse. Eric would act the part of her escort to the fullest. He would admire her dress and expect to be asked in for a drink. She wasn't sure just why she adored the ritualistic approach of the Oriental tea ceremony and disliked it intensely in Eric. She was just perverse, she supposed.

Her dress rustled, and her high-heeled sandals clicked against the wood floor as she went to open the door.

It wasn't Eric who stood there waiting to be asked in. It was Kaynon, a tall, well-groomed Kaynon, exuding a sensual appeal that was simply devastating. She felt as if she had been starved for him.

Every nerve in her body seemed to rise up and vibrate. She was too shocked to think. When her powers of reasoning did return, she was filled with an overriding sense of disaster.

"Aren't you going to ask me in?" His eyes were caressive.

"I thought you were out of town," she said stupidly.

"I was lucky. I was on standby and one of the other passengers did a no-show." His mouth quirked. "I barely had time to shower and get over here, and I was telling myself I was a fool to rush around like a maniac just for the privilege of walking into the gallery with you on my arm."

His eyes flickered over her. "And now," he said softly, "I've changed my mind." His dark green gaze traveled down the length of her throat. "You aren't very tan. Hasn't the weather been good?"

"I . . . haven't been at the lake."

He didn't move toward her, but she was so aware of him that he seemed to fill the doorway. He wore a sleek light gray suit and a white silk shirt, unbuttoned at the throat with a silvery scarf tucked ascot fashion in the opening. The lustrous shine of the fabric contrasted with the bronze tone of his throat. "If you aren't going to ask me in, I'll have to kiss you out here."

She wanted desperately to be in his arms, but she stepped away and said, "Come in." Knowing what would follow. Knowing he would hate her when he saw. . . .

He took it all in slowly, the Japanese prints at the window, the ivory collection and netsuke placed lovingly in a closed glass étagère with the spotlight glowing behind them—and the alcove with its low table, the tatami mat, and the scroll she had hung to replace the *ikebana*.

"I've never," he said slowly, deliberately, "had the urge to wrap my hands around a woman's neck and squeeze— quite like I do right now."

"I wanted to explain," she said. "I tried to that night you talked about the tea ceremony."

"But you didn't quite make it, did you?" He reached out and grasped her arm. "You were too busy trying to seduce me." He loosened his hold and pushed her away from him. She stumbled and nearly fell, and he caught her elbow. "Thank God you didn't succeed."

That stung. She faced him, her eyes blazing. "If you'd let me explain instead of hurling accusations at me—"

His attractive mouth drew down. "What's to explain? You're a lovely little liar—if not in words, in actions, surely."

"You're exaggerating this all out of proportion," she said sharply. "Suppose I did happen to know all the things you told me. What difference does it make?" Oh, God, if only he would take her in his arms and say, *none, none at all.*

"The difference is that I've bared my soul to you on several occasions—and you've hidden the most important part of your life from me."

The words wounded and sliced and left her with only her pride. She raised her chin and told the lie with style and fury. "I couldn't care less what you think of me." Echoes of quarrels with Bryant chimed through her, echoing like bells.

His eyes glittered. "No, you couldn't, could you?" His lashes flickered and he took a step toward her. She had all she could do to keep from shrinking away. "But now that we know where we stand, we're much better off."

His tone frightened her, but she wasn't going to let him know that. "I . . . don't know what you mean."

"Oh, I think you do." He pulled her into his arms, and slowly, his eyes riveted on her face, he watched for the minutest betrayal of emotion. She knew what he must be seeing, furious little lights in the brown depths of her eyes, a mouth that trembled with conflicting urges, the long, taut curve of her throat as she lifted her head to meet his derisive stare. For a tense, aching moment, he merely watched. Then, as if satisfied that he had kept her in suspense long enough, he smiled, a sardonic lift of the lips. She should have broken away from him then, but she had lost the power to move. She waited—as if mesmerized by the sight of her own destruction. He strung out the waiting, slowly lowering his head. At last his lips took hers, covered her mouth in a way that conveyed every ounce of his cool contempt.

She tried not to respond, tried not to let him feel the wild elation that made her tremble, but he was a man with a knowledge of women, and he knew he was turning her bones to water with those persuasive, knowing lips. She had missed him desperately, and now, to have that warm mouth covering hers, that tongue probing insistently, taking the sweetness that she wanted, needed to give, destroyed every defense she had. She surrendered, reaching under his jacket to put her hands on his back, glorying in the sensation of his chest pressing against her breasts. She wore no bra, and she could feel his heart pounding against her own, throbbing with vibrant life. She leaned back, allowing him the access to her mouth he demanded. His lips lifted from hers, only to feather over her jaw, the curve of her throat, and down to the sensitive hollow. His hands moved over her back and down to her lower hips and lower still to the full curves, cupping them insolently.

"I was going to be so careful with you," he murmured,

raising his mouth to her ear. "I was going to go slowly, let you be sure, treat you with such tender loving care." His hand moved upward along her spine and around to the top of her belt, just under her breast. "But now I won't have to do that, will I? Now we know exactly what we want from each other."

"I—don't want anything from you." She forced the words out and tried to push him away with the hands that had so recently betrayed her.

He gave her a mocking smile and slowly loosened his grip on her back. "I think by the end of the evening you will tell me something quite different," he said smoothly, an undertone of menace in the words as he stepped away. "But for now, we do have other obligations, don't we?"

He waved a hand toward the door with a mocking deference that gave her a small preview of what the rest of the evening would be like. "I've changed my mind," she said huskily. "I'm not going."

Quick as lightning, his mood shifted. He was violently angry, and his anger had its only outlet in the hand he whipped out and wrapped around her wrist. "You're going with me, Miss Hallworth. An art connoisseur like yourself will be a worthy addition to our small but elite group."

"You can't force me to go—"

He thought about that. Then he let her go, a strange glittering light in his eyes. "No, I can't." His hand went to the one button that held his jacket closed. He unbuttoned it, watching her. "As a matter of fact, I'd much rather spend the evening here . . . with you."

She whirled around and grabbed her off-white shawl from the back of the couch and walked to the door.

"Somehow I had a feeling you'd change your mind," he murmured as he followed her out the door.

The gallery, an old Victorian house on East Avenue that Bruce Edwards had converted some thirty years ago, was brightly lit. The curving bay on the second story glowed, and even the "widow's watch," that turreted tower on the third floor with its circular windows, sent out a soft gleam. On the ground level, lights blazed through the open double doors, giving the impression of warmth and gaiety within. She hoped it wasn't a false impression. She needed some warmth and gaiety. Kaynon had not said a word during the entire trip. His silence chilled her blood, locked away any words of explanation inside her brain.

Bruce Edwards came to meet them the moment they stepped inside the door. He was a tall, slender man who looked more like Eric than he did Kaynon. "There you are. I hoped you would arrive before Lucille got here. Have a good trip, son?"

"Not too bad. Right now I could use a drink. Eric tending bar?"

"We hired a lad from one of the motels. There's wine punch, if you'd like something sweet. Speaking of sweet things, how are you, my dear?" He offered his cheek, and she leaned forward and kissed it. It felt warm and smooth.

"Fine. Thank you for inviting me."

"Knew you wouldn't want to miss it." He glanced at Kaynon, who stared back at him with a bland look. "Why don't you take Tarra around, son? Show her some of our new stuff. She hasn't been here in ages."

"So she said." He smiled at her now, all charm and smooth male politeness. "I'd be glad to show her around."

The house had an open floor plan. The entryway led into an elegant drawing room that contained no furniture, but instead, was highlighted by a shiny oak wood floor and wainscoting going halfway up the wall. Above the intricate chair rail, works by French masters hung on the white wall. There was a Degas, his ballerinas in the act of readying themselves for a performance, their dresses gauzy, their bodies bent away from the viewer as if they were peering around the stage curtain. There was a Van Gogh, a Monet. All, or nearly all, of the paintings were familiar to her.

"This is the room given over to the French Impressionists," he said in her ear, his voice deep, his tone mocking. "I'm sure you would rather move along to the area of your interest."

He took her elbow and steered her past an elegant-looking woman in a short rose chiffon gown, who was deep in conversation with Peter Goodson, the fortyish, dapper art critic whose articles appeared in the *Times Union*. Peter spied her and broke off in mid-sentence. "Tarra, darling. How are you?"

"Fine, thank you," she said, hoping she sounded suitably casual and not as strung-up as she felt. "How are you, Peter?"

"Better now that I've seen you. Vacation nearly over?"

"I have another week."

"We'll get together for lunch when you come back. I'll call you."

"I'll look forward to it," she said, aware with every particle in her body of the taut fingers of the man who held her elbow in an ever-tighter grip.

When they moved away, he rasped, "There's no end to the things I'm learning about you tonight, is there?"

She knew it wouldn't do any good to defend herself, but she felt compelled to try. "He's a good friend, nothing more. He and my father golf together."

"How convenient," he said, but she knew he didn't believe her.

She said, "I thought you wanted a drink." His hard fingers seemed to be permanently attached to the joint of her elbow in a way that was not exactly painful, but confining, forcing her to walk in the direction he wanted her to go.

"I'll get one later," he murmured. "Right now, I've promised to give you a tour of the gallery."

He guided her toward the arched doorway. At the crown of the arch hung the lettered sign Treasures of the Orient, and directly ahead of her was the Kwan shai-yin seated on his pedestal, his feet at her eye level, one knee lifted, his wrist draped elegantly over it.

"You'll forgive me," Kaynon said, his voice low and mocking, "but since I had my lecture all planned, I'll go ahead and give it anyway. You won't be too bored, will you?" The words were pointed, each one a tiny sword thrust.

"Kaynon—"

"This is a Sung dynasty figure, a bodhisattva, a being chosen for enlightenment who has forsaken nirvana in order to save others. My namesake, strangely enough."

"The Lord Who Looks Down with Mercy," she murmured.

He lifted an eyebrow. "Are you finding it something of a misnomer?"

"Yes," she said. "Will you let go of me?"

He ignored her. "If you stand here, you'll find that he looks directly at you." He positioned her in front of the statue, and in spite of herself, she looked up. Those dark eyes staring directly into her own gave her a distinct jolt.

"Disconcerting, isn't it?" he said almost conversationally. "Kwanyin is reminding you, perhaps, that you have to be worthy of the mercy he offers. Unlike the later portraits of the nineteenth century, however, his eyes will not follow you around the room. Once you remove yourself from his gaze, he forgets you."

"Kaynon, please. It isn't necessary to—"

In answer, he pushed her further into the room, taking her to the freestanding Plexiglas display case. "And here we have a T'ang horse in cream glaze, possibly the most valuable article in this room, even though it is only sixteen inches high. But I know you must already be aware of the T'ang dynasty—when court painters were called upon to paint portraits of the imperial horses, and small miniatures of the noble beasts were hawked along the roadside to passing funeral processions, since no self-respecting warrior could be buried without a figure of a horse. But then, of course," his voice carried that mocking, sardonic tone she had come to dread, "you already know all these things, don't you?"

She looked at the biscuit-colored horse. Through long habit, and to distract herself from the pain of Kaynon's needling comments, she studied every detail. Its glaze was speckled with cracking, as most authentic specimens of that age and type were, yet the sheen of the expert Chinese glazing was still visible. The base was a deep brown color. "Look at everything carefully," she could hear her father saying. "The only way a connoisseur really learns to tell the fake from the real even in this day of infrared rays and carbon dating is by looking, looking, looking, and holding it in your hand—if possible." And Kaynon's voice: "But the best test of anything is how it feels in your hands." . . . She saw it then, the tiny imperfection on the dark base just to the front of the horse's back left foot that would make this horse individual and unique from any others.

He said, "Or could I draw your attention to this ink-drawn hanging scroll?" pulling her around to face the wall, "One monkey is daring enough to reach for the moon, while the other merely drops his arm toward the water—to the lovely reflection, that empty gossamer substitute for the real thing." His eyes moved over her face, and she knew he was comparing her to that empty reflection.

"There you are, Tarra." Eric sauntered toward her, his tall, slim body clad in a black velvet evening jacket and dark trousers, his shirt white and crisp with ruffles. He cast a quick, flickering look at his brother and said, "You found her apartment all right then."

"Yes," Kaynon drawled. "I found it."

"Darling, come and have some wine punch." Eric took hold of her arm, and Kaynon's hand fell away from her instantly. Why did one man's touch have the power to warm her to the tips of her toes, while another's felt as cool and dry as leaves in the fall? It should have been a relief to walk away from Kaynon. Then why did she feel so bleak inside?

She listened with half her attention to Eric's explanation of the last-minute crisis that had forced him to send Kaynon in his stead and his enthusiastic account of the collection that Mrs. Stratton-Duncan had agreed to donate to the gallery. As they stopped in front of the punch bowl and he ladled some of the shimmering, clear liquid out for her, he enumerated them. "A Bramantino *Madonna with Child and Two Angels,* a George Inness *July Moonrise in Florida,* and a Picasso *Flowers in a Blue Vase.*"

"I'm glad," she murmured, taking the cup from him.

A couple, she in a lime-green dress of expensive cut and color, he in a custom-fitted suit, walked in the door. She knew them well; they were friends of her parents, and they contributed much of their wealth and their time to the promotion of art in the city. The gallery was almost filled with people similar to the Blakes, people who believed in the place of art in their lives.

A small group of musicians began to play soft music just as Kaynon strolled out of the room where she had left him—with Pamela on his arm. She wore black tonight, a one-shouldered dress that bared a large triangle of tanned skin and the tantalizing glimpse of a rounded breast. The skirt came just to her knees and swirled around her lovely legs, and she wore sandals. Her hips swayed enticingly as she walked beside Kaynon and laughed up into his face, eyes vivid and sparkling. The most disconcerting thing of all was that they were headed straight toward the punch table.

"The lady with Kaynon Edwards looks familiar. Is she his current love?"

Tarra turned. Peter was at her elbow, his face urbanely smooth. She laughed, but even to her ears the nervous edge was audible. "Why don't you ask him?"

"I just might," Peter drawled.

Eric said in a cool voice, "She happens to be my secretary, Pamela Wilson."

"Lovely woman. Edwards has good taste."

"I didn't know you included personal tidbits in your column," Eric said.

Peter gave him a bland look. "Anything Kaynon Edwards does is news. He's something of a celebrity—in art circles, at least."

"Is he?" Eric countered, turning his head to look at his brother walk across the room toward them. "Notorious would describe it better, I should think."

"Do I detect a touch of Cain and Abel here?" Peter asked, his eyebrows raising as he turned to focus his gaze on Eric.

Eric frowned, his eyes dark. "Not from me, you don't." He wasn't happy. His mouth took on a sullen look. "Go somewhere else to dig out your melodramatic stories."

Peter laughed, a low chuckle. "You know what your trouble is? You have no sense of humor."

"It's nothing to joke about," Eric said stiffly. "I've heard how wonderful my brother is for years. It's only a miracle I haven't killed him long ago."

CHAPTER FIVE

Peter looked taken aback, and when Eric walked out from behind the table, gave him a black look, and stalked away, he shook his head in amazement. "Thin-skinned, isn't he?"

"He had difficulty getting things arranged tonight, and he's probably a little tense," she explained, justifying Eric's show of temper, knowing that Eric had told the truth when he said he'd heard about Kaynon for years. Bruce Edwards had often been less than tactful in front of his eldest son. In the time when Kaynon was in high school and college, Bruce had been too proud of Kaynon's athletic accomplishments, too prone to give times and days and dates of Kaynon's victories. Perhaps, Tarra thought belatedly, thinking of what Kaynon had told her, Bruce Edwards had also been perversely proud of his youngest son's refusal to be dominated by his father.

"Something eating him?" Kaynon asked, watching Eric walk away, his eyes cool, his face unreadable, Pamela clinging to his arm. She looked like an appendage, she was so close.

"Just a joke he didn't like," Peter said smoothly.

Kaynon picked up the ladle, filled a cup, and handed it to Pamela, disengaging his arm from her grip in the process. When he had filled one for himself, he said to Peter, "Enjoying yourself?"

Tarra heard the irritated edge under the words, but Peter didn't seem to. She moved nervously, nearly spilling

88

her drink. First one brother, then the other. Peter would get a complex.

"Yes, as a matter of fact I am." Peter had a full head of silvery hair that was a sign of his mature years, but he ran and played golf, and he was in good condition. His jacket fitted him smoothly. There was no bulge of middle age around his waist.

Kaynon asked, "Are you here in an official capacity or merely as a friend of the gallery?"

Tarra held her breath. As public relations liaison, Kaynon could ill afford to annoy Peter.

"Some of both, I might say. What's the matter? Didn't you see my name on the invitation list?" Peter had definitely caught the antagonism now, and he was reacting to it.

"Now that you mention it," he gazed at Peter steadily, "I didn't."

"But you've been out of town," Tarra said quickly to Kaynon.

"Yes," Kaynon murmured, looking at her. "I have been —and of course, a lot could have happened while I was gone." He looked pointedly at Peter and then at her. Was she the only one who heard the soft innuendo in his words? She fervently hoped so.

Pamela had been sipping her punch, but now she lowered her cup and said, "Peter's name automatically goes on the guest list of any function the gallery has. I distinctly remember typing one out for you and leaving it on your desk."

Kaynon swung around to her. Beneath his long lashes, his eyes gleamed. "Then it must still be there. I haven't been to my office since I got back in town."

"Umm and I've missed you too," she told him, setting her cup down and taking his arm again. "This place is a dead bore when you're gone."

"Hard to believe you got along all those years without me," Kaynon said dryly, and the irony in his voice slid right over her head. She took his words at face value. Pamela wasn't perceptive. She heard only what she wanted to hear.

"Yes, isn't it?" she said, smiling up at him, displaying even, white teeth.

Tarra's stomach churned. Somehow she had forgotten that Pamela would see him every day here at the gallery. They had evidently become much closer since that night she had danced so wantonly with him. Pamela was only slightly less blatant than she had been then—and she had given Tarra a headache. What part of Tarra's anatomy would hurt at the end of this evening?

Your heart, her mind whispered.

"Heard anything from your parents?" Peter had turned to her and was regarding her with a quizzical light of heightened interest in his eye. She couldn't let him sense the disturbed state of her thoughts. He had known her for years. He would guess the reason quick as lightning.

"Yes. They're in Switzerland. Mother called the other evening. It was good to hear her voice, and we had an excellent connection. By satellite, she said."

"Have they found anything exciting?"

She was forced then to tell him about the terra-cotta figures her mother had found. She felt Kaynon watching her. She was conscious of the slightest movement he made, from the mocking lift of his lips to the easy way he held his body, the flap of his still-loosened jacket tucked behind the hand he had shoved in his pants pocket. The compelling male magnetism that was such a part of him seemed to be reaching out and drawing her closer. For something to do, she walked around the table and helped herself to more punch as she talked. Peter watched her with a much more attentive gaze than she wanted or deserved.

She stopped talking and sipped at her drink. It was cool and tart and eased the ache in her throat. "Sounds like quite a find." Peter smiled. "Your mother always was the lucky one."

"She is intuitive. Dad calls her his witch. She sometimes gets carried away, though. She needs his steadying hand."

"And a very educated hand it is. If you've learned half of what your father knows about art, you've learned ten times more than most of the people in this business," Peter said warmly.

He meant it as a compliment to her father, but she would have preferred that he hadn't said it in front of Kaynon. It only drove the knife deeper. Kaynon's sardonic smile broadened.

"Our resident expert," he said, lifting his cup in an ersatz toast.

Peter frowned. He opened his mouth as if he were going to protest, looked at Tarra's face, and closed it.

The music changed subtly. Tarra turned to see that the floor had been cleared and people were dancing.

"Where's the guest of honor?" Pamela said languidly. "I was looking forward to seeing a lady who has ten million dollars."

"If you're talking about Mrs. Stratton-Duncan, you'll be lucky if you notice her at all," Peter told her. "She's quite ordinary looking, and she'll probably drift in and out before very many people realize she was here . . . I'd guess within the next hour or so."

"What's the fun of being rich if you can't enjoy it?" Pamela asked.

"Maybe she is enjoying it," Kaynon countered. "She's living life her way."

"Like you do," Pamela said, smiling at him.

"I have certain—constraints just like anyone else," Kaynon said coolly.

"Tarra, it isn't often I get an opportunity to hold a beautiful woman in my arms and move around the floor to music from my era. Come dance with me." Peter took her cup from her hand and set it on the table.

She murmured an affirmative answer, turned, and led the way toward the dancing couples. Out on the floor

Peter took her in his arms with the easy grace of a man with long experience of women, and said, "Eric's secretary may be beautiful, but she wears on a person very quickly. Is she always so . . . obvious?"

"Jealous?" she said lightly, teasing.

"Oh, absolutely," he said dryly.

He turned to her, and for the first time since she had opened the door and found Kaynon standing there, she relaxed. It was pleasant, drifting slowly around the floor with an undemanding man holding her, and she let her body give in and be directed by Peter's hand at the back of her waist.

"That's better. You were strung-up like a high-tension wire, my love. Do I detect undercurrents between you and Edwards?"

She was jarred, but she tried not to show it. "Still looking for a good story?" she fenced.

"Would I find one?"

"No."

"But you'd prefer I didn't go looking."

"Where's the light of your life tonight?" she asked, knowing he wouldn't be fooled by her artful conversational switch.

"Marilyn? Rehearsing for another musical, what else?"

"Her dancing must restrict your evenings together." Marilyn Weston was in her thirties, actively pursuing her dancing career. Peter wanted to marry her, but she had been putting him off.

"We manage to find some time for ourselves here and there," he said lightly. "My job takes me out in the evenings, too. If I had a nine-to-five occupation, we'd never see each other, I suppose."

The music ended, and because Peter was slow to release her from his arms, they were still standing together when the couple next to them turned. It was the Blakes, and Laura Blake greeted Peter warmly. "Peter, how are you? And how is Marilyn?"

She stepped away from Peter's arms—and saw them then, Kaynon and Pamela. They had been dancing together, but she had not seen them before. Peter must have tactfully kept her turned away from them during the entire dance. It was thoughtful of him, but now the shock of seeing them together washed over her. There was none of Kaynon's disdainful scorn in the way he was holding Pamela tonight. They, unlike Peter and herself, had not moved apart when the music ended. Kaynon's tanned fingers pressed against the black silk at the small of Pamela's back, just at the same low, erotic spot he had caressed Tarra that day on the dock. Pamela had her head back, her eyes closed. Tarra could almost feel the sensual pleasure running through the other woman. Pamela's tawny hair streamed down her half-naked back, and her fingertips were clutching Kaynon's shoulders.

Tarra clenched her hands, the memory of Kaynon's caress careening through her own body. She stood mesmerized, unable to look away. Her hands turned icy, her cheeks cool, as if the blood had left them. God, she couldn't let herself feel this way. She didn't want to care. Kaynon was far too dangerous to her peace of mind. But she couldn't call back the feelings he had aroused in her. Feelings? It was stronger than that, this emotion that rose up in her like hot molten lava. Instinctively, her mind recognized the truth—and rebelled. No! She couldn't be falling in love, not again. He was all wrong for her. He hated her. She took a step forward, and into her direct line of vision Bryant walked, with a sultry dark-haired beauty clinging to his arm. Behind them stood Lucille Stratton-Duncan, looking around in a rather lost way, as if she were unsure of what she should do, wearing a nondescript dress of pale beige that hung on her thin body indifferently. The woman with Bryant gave Mrs. Stratton-Duncan a dazzling smile, and it was then that Tarra remembered who Bryant's lady friend was. The sultry beauty was Carla Redbourn, a niece of the wealthy woman.

"Hello, Tarra."

Bryant had walked the few steps it took to bring him directly in front of her, and at the same time, Kaynon released Pamela.

Conscious of Kaynon's eyes on her, she forced a smile to her lips and said, "Hello, Bryant." She was still reeling from the shock of revelation that seeing Kaynon in Pamela's arms had given her. She felt almost incapable of dealing with anything, and something about the look on Bryant's face told her he enjoyed having her see him in the company of another beautiful woman. Carla was just his style, with good connections and wealth to back her beauty. Tarra felt nothing. He could have walked in with ten beauty queens for all she cared. She wished him luck with this one. He would need it.

Her head went up, and her eyes met Bryant's steadily. He was dressed in a pale cream suit that complemented his blond hair. He knew how good-looking he was, and he dressed accordingly. His clothes were always impeccable.

She couldn't keep the faint touch of irony out of her voice. "Fancy meeting you here."

His eyes glinted with anger, but he said easily, "Carla promised her aunt she would come along and give her moral support this evening. I decided to tag along."

"How thoughtful of you."

"Darling?" Carla's voice didn't match her looks. It grated on the nerves, was a shade too high in pitch. "Introduce me."

"Tarra Hallworth, Carla Redbourn."

"Tarra?" One dark, well-shaped eyebrow raised. The girl wore a low-cut taffeta blouse in a deep rose color and a full black skirt that rustled slightly at her least movement. "Isn't she your—"

Bryant shook his head impatiently, and the color Tarra had lost came flooding back into her cheeks. "It was nice to meet you, Miss Redbourn," she said, lying through her

94

teeth. "If you'll excuse me—I was just on my way upstairs."

She fled across the floor, cursing herself for a fool. As if the gods were condemning her, she saw Kaynon watching her, even while Pamela stood with her arm around him, her fingers caressing his nape.

The powder room was on the second floor. Flushed, breathless, she found the door at the end of a long hall. Since she had been there, it had been remodeled with big wall-length mirrors and decorative faucets.

She gazed at herself in the mirror, seeing the pain in her brown eyes. She had told herself Kaynon was far too intelligent to fall for Pamela's wiles, but she had been wrong. She had been wrong about Bryant, and she was wrong about Kaynon.

She would forget him; she had to. She would put him out of her mind, and after tonight she would make sure that she didn't come into contact with him again. That probably wouldn't be too hard. He would be seeing Pamela.

She walked out of the ladies' room, determined to hold her head high no matter what Kaynon did, when she saw him. He stood at the end of the hall, the light shining on his dark auburn hair. She couldn't see his face in the dim light, but the tension in his body communicated itself to her as she walked toward him.

"Have you decided to come out of hiding?"

"I wasn't . . . hiding." She stepped closer and turned to go down the stairs.

He caught her back with a hard hand on her elbow. "I want to talk to you."

She tensed, knowing he was going to tell her he wanted to take Pamela home. "Well?" she said, lifting her chin, her brown eyes flashing.

He looked down at her and then gave her a little push toward the other set of stairs that went up. "Not here. Let's go up to the tower."

95

She made a soft sound of protest, but his hand on her arm tightened, and unless she wanted to make a scene, which she didn't, there was nothing she could do but precede him up the stairs.

She came out of the stairwell into a small circular room. The windows dominated; they were uncurtained and gave a gorgeous view of the city, a contrast of dark shapes of trees and lighted skyscrapers. Paintings hung between the windows, all bound by a central theme, the theme of waiting—two musicians waiting to play; a woman standing by the side of the road, her hands shading her eyes, her body strained, looking; a child watching his mother cut a birthday cake. In the center was a statue, the head and torso of a young Greek man.

As if the waiting of those in the pictures had affected her thoughts, she stood looking out the window, her heart thumping with nervous anticipation, conscious of his hard male body beside her. Its perfection, though clothed, was as compelling as the statue he stood beside.

Driven to distraction by her thoughts, she said, "Well? Why did you want to talk to me?" She steeled herself, waiting for him to explain he was going to take Pamela home.

"Stop acting like a jealous little fool."

She stood in shocked silence, trying to gather up her shattered poise. Dear God. He knew she loved him—and he was angry.

She struggled to regain the breath that had been knocked from her lungs. He had seen her face, and he didn't like it. She groped for something to say and could only say the obvious. "I'm sorry. I—it isn't something I can—control."

"For God's sake." He grabbed her upper arms and gave her an impatient little shake. "He's not worth it, can't you see that?"

Startled, she fought to maintain her mental balance. "I—I don't know what you mean."

"You should. You were married to him once. You should know by now that Reece isn't worth one second of your time."

Head reeling, she tried to think. She felt lost in the tortuous path of his words. But gradually, she began to understand. He hadn't known she was jealous of Pamela. He thought the look on her face was caused by Bryant's entrance with a beautiful woman.

Relief sang through her. Cautiously, she said, "I suppose that's true."

His grip tightened, but not to the point of hurting her. "Of course it's true, you little fool."

Her mind working like lightning, she looked up at him. "Why should you care?"

He stared down at her, the dim light in the room obscuring the expression on his face. "My God." The words sounded as if he had to drag them from his throat. "You know the answer to that."

He pulled her into his arms, and there in the softly lit circular room he kissed her. His mouth and body robbed her of the will to resist. She let his lips move over hers, savoring the feel of his mouth discovering the taste and texture of hers. His tongue probed beyond her teeth to find the sensitive warmness that waited for him. He possessed her with his mouth and hands, and she didn't deny his possession. She burrowed under his jacket, between the silky lining and the sleek shirt. She remembered what he had looked like walking away in his swimming trunks that day on the dock and how she had wanted to touch his naked back as he had touched hers. She ached to mold his torso with her hands, discover the fine lines of him as she might have a work of art. . . .

He lifted his mouth from hers. "I can help you forget him."

"I don't need—"

"No." He put his finger over her mouth, and his gentle touch on her lips sent new sensations running through her.

"Don't excuse or prevaricate or deny. You want me just as much as I want you."

An undefined emotion welled up in her. Yes, she wanted him. But she loved him, too. All he felt for her was physical need.

"I'm not ready to—get involved with anyone just yet."

His body stiffened as if she had hit him. He released her as if he no longer wanted to touch her. "You still love him, don't you?"

A vehement denial would have him wondering why she had paled before, downstairs. His quick mind might jump around and come up with the right answer. "I suppose that I'll . . . always . . . care for him in a certain way."

"In every damn way there is, you mean." She didn't deny it, and his normally taut body seemed to tense even more. "He's no longer your husband; he's here with another woman. If you have any sense at all, you'll stop sulking like a spoiled child and come downstairs with me."

She couldn't spend a whole evening pretending she was in love with Bryant. "And then what, fade into the wall?"

"No, we'll stay together," he shot back coolly. He paused and then shadowed his eyes with a quick sweep of his lashes. "We'll dance, as if we were—lovers."

She thought of Pamela in his arms, and said, "I can't . . . do that."

He shackled her wrist with his hard grip. "You can and you will. And just to make sure there's no doubt about what we've been doing up here—" He jerked her into his arms and kissed her, a hard bruising kiss on the lips. When she thought she was going to suffocate under the relentless pressure of that mouth, he released her and half pushed, half dragged her down the stairs. At the bottom she followed him to the edge of the dancing area. There he pulled her into his arms with a rough possession. Oh, God, it was heaven and hell to be in his arms like this.

He said, "Smile and look at me." Numbly she did as he

asked, wondering at the cause of those dancing little lights in his eyes. He pulled her closer, and the palm of his hand seemed made to fit into the small of her back. She forgot that a world outside Kaynon's arms existed. His hips moved against hers as intimately as a lover's, and his thigh brushed her own sensuously. His nearness launched a subtle invasion and she had no defense against him.

"Damn it, relax. Is pretending you have some feeling for me so damn hard?"

"No," she murmured, knowing she was lying, knowing that it was infinitely hard—but not for the reasons he imagined.

"You dance well."

"So do you," she answered, hoping desperately he couldn't feel the thud of her heart through the thin material of her dress.

The music ended, but he did not immediately release her from his arms. He held her close, just as he had Pamela.

She was facing away from the crowd, but the click of high heels on the wood floor warned her.

"Kaynon?" Pamela stood beside them, flashing him her most beguiling smile. "Save the next dance for me, won't you?" He stared at her, not answering, and in the sudden quiet, she said, "You will, won't you?" Her words seemed to fall into the silence like stones in a pool.

"I'm sorry," Kaynon said. His voice was lower, but it held a note of cold warning that carried to every corner of the room. "I'm taking Tarra home."

"Leaving so soon? But it's still early." She laughed, a low, throaty chuckle that conveyed just the right amount of sexual innuendo, her eyes glittering as she looked at Tarra.

The appalled silence seemed to grow and swell and have a life of its own.

Pamela put out her hand and stroked his jacketed arm

just above the elbow, her eyes slanted up at him from under long, dark lashes. "Have fun."

With a slow, deliberate motion, he stepped away from Pamela's grasp and took Tarra's hand in his own. "I intend to," he murmured silkily.

Facing Tarra, he asked, "Shall we?"

"Yes," she murmured, her own cheeks burning.

"I'll get your shawl."

Her cheeks were hot when he helped her into the car, but the memory of Pamela's angry face staring at them in that instant before they walked away made a chill shiver over her. She pulled her shawl up over her shoulders and sat back in the seat.

"Are you cold? If you are, I can start the heater—"

"No, I'm all right."

He glanced at her once and then returned his attention to the street.

At her door he pulled her close and kissed her. "When are you going back down to the cottage?"

"Tomorrow morning."

"I may not make it down right away, but I'll come soon." He kissed her again and then lifted his mouth and caught the lobe of her ear in his teeth. His lips and tongue stroked and caressed that sensitive part of her body in a way that was erotic and possessive and utterly disturbing. She trembled in reaction, and he laughed softly. "You can depend on it."

In bed later the promise in the soft laugh made her tremble. She was filled with pictures of him, lovely erotic pictures of Kaynon sliding the straps of her chiffon nightgown off her shoulders, Kaynon kissing her mouth, her throat, her breasts, his hands discovering her. . . .

The next morning the phone woke her. It was Dede, sounding thoroughly miserable. "I've got a summer cold. That was why I couldn't come last night. Did you have a good time?"

"I'm not exactly sure you could call it that."

"What happened?"

Tarra told her about Bryant's appearance, and about Pamela's possessiveness just as she and Kaynon were leaving.

Dede groaned. "I'll be out of work till Tuesday at least, and Pam will have to pick up my work as well as her own. She'll be mad as a hornet when I get back. God only knows what she'll do. Remember what I said and be careful."

"I'll remember," she assured the other girl, thinking Dede had an overactive imagination.

Dede asked, "How did you like the gallery? They've added a lot, haven't they? Did you see the T'ang horse? Isn't he a beauty? He is my absolute favorite. I look at him every day and eat my heart out."

"He's gorgeous all right," Tara agreed. "Much more elegant than mine."

"Oh, I didn't mean that," Dede said hastily. "I just—I don't know. There's something about this one that fascinates me. The horse seems so—strong and I know it's so old and I look at it and shivers go down my spine."

"There's no reason you shouldn't admire it," Tarra assured her. "That ancient Chinese artist did a beautiful job."

Dede answered by sneezing into the phone.

"Bless you. Is there anything I can do for you? Bring over some chicken soup?"

"That would be a cure worse than the sickness," Dede drawled.

"Come on. I can open a can, at least."

"No, I'm mobile. I can wield the can opener, if it comes to that. I just thought I'd better call in case you were leaving today."

"Thanks. I'll call you when I get back in town—probably Saturday or Sunday. Listen, take care of yourself. Take some vitamin C with your chicken soup."

"Anything you say, Doctor Hallworth."

Tarra laughed and hung up. Conversation with Dede always brightened her mood. She was a good friend—the best. She wondered if she should, despite Dede's protests, go over and see how she was. But that was foolish, she supposed. Dede would be better off sleeping. If Tarra went over to her apartment, it would be just like Dede to get up and fix lunch for them both.

She packed the car with the few necessities she would need, stopped at the store and bought a comic get-well card for Dede, mailed it, and took the exit to the expressway.

She hadn't slept well the night before—something that seemed to happen all too frequently since she met Kaynon Edwards—and by the time she had driven to the cottage, unpacked, and checked the refrigerator to see if there was something cold she could have for dinner, she was more than ready to put on her swimsuit and go out on the dock to lie in the sun and spend a lazy Sunday afternoon.

On Monday morning Kaynon Edwards walked into his office and shrugged out of his jacket. He had a list of two hundred names to go over, people who should be approached either in person or by phone and asked to support the gallery. He had to check the printer's proofs of some publicity releases, and he had to contact the president of the Women's League and begin to make arrangements for Kaleidoscope.

"I was beginning to wonder if you were going to make it."

Eric stood in the door, his eyes watchful under the dark brows.

Kaynon sat down in the black swivel chair and looked up at him. "I wasn't aware I was punching a time clock."

"You aren't," Eric said shortly. "I thought you might not make it at all this morning. I heard you pacing the floor last night and wondered what was wrong."

"I wasn't sick. I was thinking."

"I can guess what you were thinking about. Come to any conclusions?" Eric's mouth twisted.

Kaynon met his sharp gaze. "No."

Eric said bluntly, "Leave Tarra alone."

Kaynon swayed back in the chair, his eyes narrowed. "Are you in love with her?"

"I want to marry her. She would make an ideal wife."

"Fit right into an empty little slot in your carefully arranged life, you mean."

Eric's face darkened. "I happen to love her."

"You have a strange way of showing it. When it comes to a choice between her and the gallery, you choose the gallery."

"Tarra understands."

"Maybe she understands because she doesn't give a damn. Maybe she's carrying the torch for another man."

"Reece? I don't think so."

Kaynon was silent, his long fingers restlessly drumming on the dark green desk blotter. "You want me to back off?"

Red color rushed to Eric's face. "Don't do me any favors."

Kaynon's hands dropped from the desk. "What the hell do you want from me? Do you want me to leave you a clear field, or do we call it every man for himself?"

"I'm not blind. I know she's attracted to you. I'm not giving you the added advantage of making you forbidden fruit."

He twisted out of the swivel chair, and walked to the window, his back to Eric. "I'm sorry that life handed you a raw deal, Brother. But I . . . can't give in to you on this one."

"I don't want you to." Eric's voice sounded husky. "We'll leave it to Tarra to make the choice."

Kaynon turned. "Fair enough."

"Just don't hurt her," Eric said grittily. "She's been through enough."

"I don't intend to," Kaynon said quietly.

"She's not the love and leave 'em kind."

Kaynon stared at Eric. "I know that—"

The sound of footsteps in the hallway warned them they were no longer alone.

"I wondered where everyone was." Pamela looked cool and businesslike in a white linen suit with a demure pink blouse.

She glanced at Eric. "Did you have dictation you wanted me to do?"

He shook his head. "Dede Adams called in sick this morning. I think Kaynon may need you. I'll check with you this afternoon if I have anything pressing."

Eric gave them both a curt nod and left, leaving Kaynon with a vague feeling of dissatisfaction in his gut. Pamela stepped in, carrying her steno pad. She had been professional in the office, without a hint of the wanton behavior that she indulged in outside of business hours. The sly, slightly feline smile she gave him this morning was a surprise. He said, "Are you free now or shall we plan it for later this morning?"

"I'm free now." Carrying her pad, she walked with that slow, sexy walk of hers to the chair beside his desk, settled herself, and crossed her legs, tugging her skirt over her knee.

He had too much to do to play games with her this morning. He plunged into the work at once, firing off several letters to her in rapid fashion. When he was through, he gave her a list of people he wanted her to contact and arrange appointment times for him. He gave her hours and days that he would be available and warned her to keep track of the ones she made in order to avoid conflicts.

It was almost two hours before they finished.

"That's all you wanted—for now?"

The sexual innuendo was there, but he ignored it. "I think that will do it."

She went to the door and then turned. "Oh, Kaynon, Eric asked me to get your key to the cottage and have another copy made for him. He seems to have lost his."

Kaynon frowned. "He didn't say anything about it this morning."

Pamela shrugged. "I suppose it slipped his mind. If you want to speak to him about it yourself—"

He made an impatient movement and stuck his hand in his pocket to pull out his keys.

"Just leave it on your ring," she said, smiling. "I'll get it back to you in an hour—before you go out for lunch."

"I'm working through. Make sure I have them back to me by four o'clock this afternoon."

Three hours later he found the keys on his desk. Pamela had evidently returned them when he had gone upstairs for a moment. She was a good secretary. She got things done when she said she was going to. He stuck the keys in his pocket, finished going over the proofs from the printer, and decided he had had enough.

Out in the parking lot, as he was shrugging off his jacket in the summer heat and tossing it into the backseat of his car, his father drove into the gallery parking lot.

Bruce Edwards parked his silver Mercedes-Benz and climbed out to walk over to Kaynon. "Leaving, Son?"

"I'm heading down to the lake. Did you want to see me?"

"I just wondered how things were going."

"Fairly well."

His father gave him a cool, searching look. "You and Eric getting along?"

"As well as can be expected. Can I talk to you later? I wanted to get down to the lake and take a swim."

His father made a gesture with his hand. "Don't let me keep you."

Kaynon got into his car and stuck the key in the ignition

and turned. A low, dead sound was the engine's only response.

"Sounds like your battery is dead."

"Sounds like," Kaynon repeated grimly and got out of the car, slamming the door to relieve some of his anger.

"Take my car," Bruce Edwards told him, dragging his keys from the pocket of his pants. "I'll ride home with Eric."

When Kaynon hesitated, his father blustered, "Well, go on, take it. You've taken little enough from me in your life, do me the favor of taking my car—now when you need it." A smile lifted the older man's lips. "I thought you wanted to get down to the lake." The smile widened. "It's mighty hot in the city today. A cool swim would feel good."

The glint in his father's eye told Kaynon he hadn't fooled the older man about his reasons for wanting to get to the cottage. A slow smile lifted his lips. "Yeah, it would. Thanks, Dad."

CHAPTER SIX

The day before, Tarra had told herself she wasn't waiting for anything, but every time a car passed on the road she heard it.

The sky was a gorgeous blue that day, and the lake was just as beautiful, with wavelets so perfect they might have been designed by a Hollywood producer. But as the sun dropped lower in the sky and no car pulled into the driveway next door, she could take no pleasure in the beauty of the sunset.

She had lain on the dock in the fading light and told herself she didn't care, but when she finally decided that Kaynon did not intend to come to the cottage that day at all, she lost her temper and dived into the lake to cool off. Kaynon had used her to ward off Pamela, and while she could hardly blame him, she thought he might have been honest enough to admit that's what he had done, later, at her door, instead of making her think he was coming down to the cottage to be with her.

The next day, she fought off depression until suddenly, around four o'clock, she heard the familiar crunch of gravel, and her heart gave a flying leap. She was lying on the dock, wearing a bikini this time, a black one that covered just the essentials; and she stayed where she was, her sunglasses shielding her eyes, her hair wrapped in a towel. Let him find her. She wasn't going searching for him.

She was on her stomach with her eyes closed when she

heard the steps on the dock. "Permission to come aboard requested."

In utter astonishment she scrambled around and sat up—to find Peter walking down the dock toward her, his lips lifted in a smile, his graying hair blowing attractively around his head. "Peter! What are you doing here?" Goodson had rarely, if ever, visited her parents at the cottage. He made no secret of his preference for the city life. He considered their cottage rustic, barely civilized.

He had the grace to look sheepish. "Mind if I sit down?"

She patted the cushion. "Not at all. Can I get you a drink?"

"Later, perhaps, when you're ready to go in." His eyes wandered over her sleek brown body. "You look as if you're enjoying the sun. And on you it looks marvelous."

"Thank you." She waited, her curiosity rising. When he didn't say anything, she asked, "Peter, why are you here?"

"It's amazing how far a man will be driven by guilty conscience," he murmured. "Forty miles, to be exact."

"Guilty conscience?"

He grimaced. "Your mother and father asked me to keep an eye on you while they were gone."

It was her turn to make a face. "I'm a big girl now," she said lightly.

"I know. That's what I told myself. That's why I didn't do anything about watching over you. My God, I told myself, what trouble can she get into just sitting on the shore of an obnoxious little lake?"

She had to laugh at that. "You're the only one who would say that. Most people think it's a lovely little lake."

"You're distracting me," he said, smiling. "In more ways than one." His eyes flickered over her once again, and there was nothing in them to suggest he thought of himself as a surrogate father.

She stirred, uncomfortably aware that she had very little on and he was fully dressed in a natty summer suit of light gray, his tie a crisp and correct darker shade. "Does Marilyn know you're here?"

"Actually, she sent me. She has some second cousin or some damn thing who knows Pamela. You know how it is, everybody seems to know somebody who knows somebody. Well, anyway, when I recounted the charming little scene you were caught up in the other night, she insisted on my coming out to see if you were all right."

"Your Marilyn is something special—and I'm all right, really I am."

"I was sure you would be. And the worst of it is, I can't even take you out to dinner. I'm due back in the city to cover an interview with an artist at seven thirty. I hope it's cooler by then. It was damn hot in the car." He looked so ridiculous and thoroughly miserable sitting there cross-legged on the weather-beaten cushion that she took pity on him and said, "Look, come inside and I'll get you a cool drink before you have to leave."

"You mean you do have some of the trappings of civilization in this primitive place?"

She got to her feet and held out her hand. "It's not that bad. You might even learn to tolerate it if you stayed here long enough."

Standing, he peered over the side of the dock down at the water, his nose wrinkling as if he were smelling something not quite pleasant. "Smells like fish. What are all those green things down there?"

"Lakeweed," she said, laughing, giving up, grabbing his hand. "If the water wasn't so beautifully clear you wouldn't see them at all."

"That would be a great pity." He spoke with just the right ironic inflection.

"Oh, come on. You're hopeless."

She piloted him toward the house. He resisted. She flattened her palms on his back at his waist and pushed him from behind as if he were a wheelbarrow. They slipped and slid up the slight incline, laughing. It was then she heard the car pull up and the car door slam.

She pulled her hands away from Peter's back. He straightened, with a look of chagrin on his face that might have meant anything.

Kaynon, for some reason, was driving his father's large, luxurious car, and he stood for a moment, leaning against the door. Framed against the silver Mercedes-Benz, he looked strangely male, vivid—and somehow, angry. He walked down the hill toward them, his cream shirt open at the throat and tucked into light tan suit trousers, the sleeves rolled back on his tanned arms. It must be the sun that was giving his eyes that heightened glitter. *Armed and dangerous* flitted across her mind, which was ridiculous because of course Kaynon didn't carry a gun. But compared to Peter's dapper good grooming he looked primitive, earthy. He seemed to fit in exactly with the greenness of the trees, the blue sky overhead, the sound of the squirrels chattering.

"Hello," she said, wondering why she should feel that faint twinge of guilt.

"Hello." The word was as cool as a breeze off the water.

Peter greeted him. Kaynon's reply was barely civil. His eyes flickered over Tarra and moved unhurriedly down the length of her, as if he wanted to remember every inch of her—the full maturity of her breasts barely covered by the dark patches of fabric, the bare flat stomach, the long golden thighs, the shapely tanned legs.

Then he nodded and said shortly, "If you'll excuse me, I think I'll go change. It's hot in the city, and I've been looking forward to—a swim."

"The water is just right," she offered, but Kaynon had turned and was walking away from her.

"I seem to have no rapport with either of the Edwards brothers," Peter said later, holding his gin and tonic at eye level, his long legs stretched out in front of him as he sat on her couch. "I get the distinct feeling I am persona non grata for Mr. Edwards whenever I'm with you. I wonder why." He pretended to peer at his glass as if he were puzzled, when she knew he wasn't.

"Don't probe," she told him coolly. "We've both agreed that I'm a big girl now."

"But the shark is circling, my pet. I wasn't aware you had such denizens of the deep in Conesus."

"He was only using me to frighten Pamela away."

"But who are you going to use to frighten him away?"

"You," she said lightly. "Will Marilyn mind?"

"As they say, she'll have to catch me at it first." He twirled his drink thoughtfully in his hand. "How long has it been since your divorce?"

"A year."

"Are you over him?"

"Long ago. I'm not sure I ever really loved him. I should never have married him. Marvelous, my gift for hindsight." She sipped her own icy drink. She had found a terry wrap and belted it around her, covering up everything but her legs. She sat on the floor by the low table in front of Peter, watching his mobile face attempt to conceal his concern. "I suppose you think I'm ripe for an affair."

He stared at his glass thoughtfully. "I don't know what you're ripe for. I just don't want to see you get hurt again. And Edwards is a damned attractive man—any fool can see that."

She said, "He isn't the only attractive male around here," smiling at him.

"I want to warn you that flattery, especially at my age, will get you everywhere." He set his glass on the table. "I suppose I'd better run, my love. You've got my number, haven't you? You can reach me either at home or at the paper—"

"Oh, I've got your number all right," she told him, teasing. "Drink and run, that's Goodson, leave me to my primitive squalor without a backward glance."

"That's more like it," he said. "That's the Tarra I used to know, the one who always had a comeback." He pulled her to her feet and dropped a light kiss on her forehead. "Take care—you hear? Don't let the sharks get you."

"I won't." She stood in his arms for a moment, savoring his tender protection, his sensitive caring. Through the open window came a crashing sound, as if Kaynon had dropped a glass.

"My God. Is he throwing things?"

"Don't be ridiculous. He probably just dropped something."

Peter's wary glance in the direction of the other cottage was almost comical. "He sounds violent. Are you sure you're safe with him just across the way?"

"Yes, I'm safe. Now will you stop worrying and just go? I don't want you rushing to get back to the city."

After she followed him to the door and gave him another quick kiss and a hug, he left her, moving lithely up the hill toward his car.

It was still warm, and she didn't bother to change, hoping that she would be able to go for a swim later.

Around eight o'clock the sun hung low over the hills, casting a golden glow over the water. Quiet settled in around the lake, with only an occasional boat put-putting along the opposite shore. The evening was warm. Still wearing her swimsuit and robe, she went out to the dock, conscious of the fact that there were no lights in Kaynon's cottage and nothing seemed to be stirring. She thought perhaps he might be napping.

In the shadow of the boat hoist she shed her robe, slid into the water, and began to swim. The water was shallow several feet out from the dock, and she didn't go out over her head, the one concession she made to the fact she was swimming alone.

She swam several lengths parallel to the dock, moving easily through the water, exerting herself, working hard in order to force her mind to concentrate on the exercise she

112

was giving her body. The water was warm and silky and felt like heaven against her skin. For these blissful moments she wouldn't think of Peter or Kaynon Edwards or Pamela.

But after swimming several lengths she rolled over on her back. The sun had gone down, its dying rays painting the sky a velvety rose. The lake was rose too, with the deep blue underneath giving it the look of a lush painting, fuchsia and gold over cobalt-blue water. She floated on her back and turned away from the dock to tip her head and look at the dark outline of the hills against the rose horizon. *If only all of life could be like this, simple and uncomplicated and beautiful.* She longed to take this moment and suspend it permanently in time so that she would always remember the night she had floated on a lake that shone like fire. But she couldn't. The euphoria of the moment would soon be gone, and she would be back to reality again, to the reality of her life—a life that was complicated and painful.

Her mind drifted with her body. Complicated and painful. That was an accurate description of her relationship with Kaynon. Relationship. Did she have one, really? He floated in front of her mind's eye, and she remembered the way she had felt lying under him when he kissed her on the dock, and again when he held her in his arms and danced with her. A shiver crept over her skin. He had made it clear that his freedom was everything to him. He would never allow a woman to tie him down. She wasn't sure she wanted to be tied down again, either. But she didn't want a temporary affair. It would be far too painful to let Kaynon into her life and then lose him after a few short weeks.

But if he were to come to her, here, now, in this molten lake and sky, she could not deny him.

She was fantasizing, dreaming. The lake was empty of anything but her. The landscape was silent and beautiful, like a lovely work of art. Loss and emptiness swept over

113

her. It was impossible to tolerate being here alone. She turned and began to swim toward the dock.

She reached the ladder, her wet hair clinging to her eyelashes. She flipped it back impatiently and put a foot on the bottom rung and the other on the next. The air was cool after the warmth of the water, and she was coping with the shock to her system when a shadow straightened on the dock. She nearly fell backward into the water with fear and surprise.

It was Kaynon, holding out the towel for her.

She clung to the the ladder and looked up at him. "What—what are you doing?"

"Waiting for you," he said in a dark, husky tone, and held the towel open for her.

Her fingers tightened, and then she climbed the last two rungs and stepped onto the dock. The light was almost gone, and he looked like a dark, overpowering shadow, the robe spread in front of him like a cape.

She held out her hand for it, and he shook his head. He simply held the towel . . . and waited.

She stood for a second, hesitating. It was more than symbolic to step into that towel—and his waiting arms. She would be putting herself in his hands—in every way.

"Do you have trouble making a decision?" he mocked softly.

A sudden chill feathered over her skin at the husky timbre of his voice. "Well, yes—and no."

"Come here, Tarra."

There was command in his voice, but there was something else, too, that tender vulnerability that gave her an unwillingness to hurt him. She stepped forward.

He folded her into the terry cloth, and rubbed her briskly, running his hands over her back and her shoulders. The chill fled. A heated warmth seeped through her skin everywhere he touched. His arms were a warm haven she never wanted to leave.

"You little fool." The words were spoken in the same

tone he might have used on a rebellious child. "You'll catch your death of cold."

"No," she murmured, feeling like a mummy because he had wrapped her so tightly in the terry cloth. She couldn't touch or hold him, so she edged closer, nestling in his arms. "The water was warm—beautiful."

"It must have been. I thought you were never coming out."

"Have you been watching me?"

He held her away and a slow smile lifted his lips. "It was the neighborly thing to do. You were swimming alone."

His hands had stopped their brisk rubbing and now were traveling over her back, her waist, her hips, till even the terry cloth couldn't disguise their caressing intent. His mouth was next to her ear and his warm breath fanned her cheek. Then he turned her and without a word began to guide her down the dock. When they reached the end and she moved as if to walk to her cottage, he tightened his hold on her waist. "Come home with me. I have a fire going."

"I'll go and get changed—"

"No," he said, pulling her to his side and matching his steps to hers. "I'll find something you can wear."

He clamped his hand around her waist and kept her locked to his side. She could refuse to follow him, she knew that. He was holding her tightly, but there was no real force in the hand that held her. She was going with him willingly—to whatever outcome the evening might have.

When they reached the redwood steps, she picked up the end of the towel to keep from tripping on it. Her heart beat in a loud, unsteady rhythm as they climbed the stairs. The rhythm seemed to increase as he opened the door for her and then stepped aside to allow her to precede him.

The fire crackled and glowed in the living room, the only source of light. Inside the intimate, warm room, he guided her toward the hearth. Her bare feet were tickled by the soft black fur rug. "Stand here for a moment and warm yourself. I'll go pour us something to drink."

He left her, and she stood in front of the fireplace, the stone hearth warm under her toes, heat waves warming the front of her improvised robe. She turned slowly, warming herself on all sides. She had made a complete turn and was facing the fire when Kaynon returned. The flickering flames illuminated his face and the two crystal wineglasses he held in his hand.

"I know this should be brandy, but we don't seem to have any on hand. We'll have to make do with Chablis, I'm afraid."

She held the terry cloth together with one hand and reached for the glass he held out to her. "A terrible sacrifice," she said, smiling. "I'll try not to complain."

He set his glass on the mantel and pulled two cushions off the couch, positioning them in front of the fire. "Sit down."

"I'm wet," she protested, but he shook his head. "It doesn't matter." He took her glass and pushed her gently down, then, balancing both glasses in his hands, bent his legs and seated himself beside her.

"That was a neat trick. Could I see you do that again?"

"No. I doubt if I could manage it a second time. I was showing off for your benefit."

"Like you used to do when you were a kid?"

"You did notice, then."

"I tried not to. I didn't want to give you the satisfaction. I always felt sorry for Eric."

In the light of the fire she saw the involuntary tightening of his facial muscles. But when he turned to her, the look of tension was gone. "Eric could always find someone to feel sorry for him."

She studied the dark face. "You sound . . . jealous."

He met her look steadily. "Maybe I was."

She sipped the wine. "That's hard to believe."

"Why? Because superman isn't allowed to envy anyone else?"

"I think the real question is, why should he? He has all the advantages."

"No." The denial was soft, yet there was a depth of intensity that made the word shiver over her spine. "My brother has had all the advantages . . . because he has known you all his life."

The soft emphasis of each word disturbed and yet thrilled her. "Kaynon—"

"Are you playing Peter off against him? Because if you are, I'm warning you—you'd be better off with me."

She was jolted out of the haze the warmth of the fire and the wine had created. She was instantly, gloriously angry. "That's debatable."

"Just answer the question."

"You'll have to declare me a hostile witness—because I don't intend to deny it. You wouldn't believe me, anyway." She thrust the wineglass at him. "Thanks for the drink."

She made a move to get up. He reached out, but he didn't take the glass. His fingers shackled her wrist. "You're not going anywhere."

When he took the glass from her fingers with his other hand and set it down beside his own on the hearth, she twisted her wrist inside his iron grip. "Let go of me." She cursed herself for following him into the cottage. She had fallen under the spell of the sunset—woven her own fantasy around him—and been trapped.

"Why?" he said softly. "Why not stay and compare my lovemaking to Goodson's?"

She was stilled by the cold-shock wash of his words over her and then filled with revulsion. "That's a vile thing to say."

"Why deny it?" He was cool, sardonically accepting her perfidy. "I saw him kissing you."

"Is that part of your 'good neighbor' policy, to spy out of windows at me? If so, you can forget it."

"But I can't forget you—" He pulled her toward him, and the terry cloth towel fell away. Totally vulnerable, she went into his arms, conscious of her almost naked body rubbing against the rough cloth of his cotton shirt. She put out her free hand to fend him off, but he didn't kiss her. With her teetering on the edge of the cushion, off balance, he grasped it, pulled it out from under her, tossed it away, and pressed her down against the softness of the fur rug.

Pinned down, lying on her back, she struggled furiously, but his grip on her arms was like an iron trap. She gave up finally, meeting his eyes with fire in her own. He only smiled a mocking smile and looked down at her, his eyes gleaming. He held her upper arms down against the rug and took his time, letting his eyes travel over the full breasts barely covered by the triangles of crocheted string, the bare abdomen, the second tiny strip of cloth that rode just below her hipbones, the smooth roundness of her thighs gleaming brown-gold in the firelight. She had lost the power to move, her own body totally absorbed in the singing, high-wire tension that vibrated between them. While he looked at her, she was conscious of every detail about him, the dark-red sheen of his hair, the strange, half-predatory gleam in his jade eyes, the leashed strength that seemed to hold him suspended in the air over her.

She ached to have him close to her both physically and mentally. She could no longer bear to let him go on believing that she had made love to Peter and was involved with Eric—even to protect herself from his potent attraction. She reached for him. Almost as if he read her mind, he released his grip enough so that she could touch his mouth and trace around the full curves with her fingertips. "Peter is a friend of the family," she said huskily, knowing she was making herself more open and vulnerable to him than she ever had to a man since Bryant. "He has a special lady of his own." Her fingers touched the corner of his mouth.

"Eric asked me to marry him, but I refused—because I don't love him. I never have."

He made a sound in his throat, a soft sound of distress, and took her fingers into his mouth. Gently, he bit the ends of them, his white teeth coming down on the tops of her fingernails and the soft pads underneath.

She didn't try to pull her hand away, and the soft love bites changed to kisses. "Do you believe me?" she asked, raising her other hand to touch the vibrant fullness of his dark hair the color of flame.

"Oh, God," he groaned. "I want to." He turned his mouth into her hand and kissed her palm in a warm, suppliant gesture.

Her fingers lay against his cheek. Warmly stimulated by his kisses, they were sensitive to the rough texture of his skin, the firm outline of his jaw. Like a Greek statue, he was composed of good lines.

He copied her gesture, tracing the high cheekbones, the small chin, trailing his hand lower to the vulnerable hollow of her throat. His fingers lingered there, and when her body betrayed her by trembling, he bent his head and placed his lips where his fingers had been. He pushed the fur aside and found the tied strings of her bikini at her nape. With one quick movement, he untied them.

As if he knew she might protest, he lowered his mouth and pressed it against hers. It was a teasing kiss, a kiss meant to tantalize, a brushing of the lips. She put her hand on his nape to pull him closer, but he drew back. Deftly, his hands went around her and unclipped the hook of her top. He tossed it away, and in the firelight, she saw his eyes take in the creamy perfection of her breasts. His eyes seemed to have their own effect on her, tautening the rosy crests.

His eyes darkened, and he lowered his head and feathered little kisses down the valley between her breasts to the sensitive circle of her navel. His mouth on her skin sent showers of delight cascading through her. She reached out

119

to him as he bent over her, finding his nape, running her fingers through the crisp, vibrant hair.

Slowly, as if he were savoring every inch of her, he kissed the small circle of her birth scar and then explored it with his tongue. She clutched at his shoulders, trying to control the desire that surged up through her, but his mouth and tongue had only begun their onslaught. He moved upward and found the smooth rounded curve where her skin was untanned to favor it with his erotic attention. He teased and kissed and explored her with his tongue and lips, still avoiding the rosy crest that ached for his possession. He was building the fire within her, holding back, and his restraint heightened her passion and need for him. She had never known such slow, careful loving, and she ached to return the pleasure—and to feel his mouth capturing her breast.

At last, he gave her the satisfaction she craved, his lips and tongue on the responsive peak a delight and agony mingled together. She writhed under his mouth, caught between wanting him to go on forever and wanting him to end the aching emptiness that was building in her. He broke off the embrace, only to turn to her other breast and caress and explore its rounded curves—with the same shattering effect on her senses.

Her fingernails raked across his shirt, and he lifted his head. A slight smile lifted his lips. "Kiss me, Tarra."

He leaned over her, arrogantly male, supremely confident that he had aroused her. The urge to disturb him just as much as he disturbed her overrode her longing to have his lips on hers. Raising her hands to the buttons of his shirt, she said huskily, "Is this a contest?"

"It might be," he said as she raked her nails over his skin and went on unbuttoning his shirt. "It might be a contest for survival."

She finished her task and pulled his shirt away from the waistband of his denim pants.

He watched her, his eyes shadowed by the dark, the

firelight making his hair glow with red. "I asked you to kiss me," he said huskily.

"Yes—but you didn't say where."

She pressed him down on his back on the fur rug and leaned over him. He was primitive and beautiful and male, and she only hoped she could give him half the pleasure he had given her. She bent and kissed his chest, her heart thudding as she gloried in the freedom he was giving her to explore his body. She had never felt this way with Bryant, never taken the initiative, never been allowed to express her own love. Love. Was that what this was, this heavenly delight to give and take without worry, without that vague sense of dissatisfaction she had always felt after making love with her husband? But she hadn't loved him, she knew that now. Kaynon had been there, in her mind, the ideal man she had vaguely dreamed about but never encountered. That was what had disturbed her the first night she saw him . . . she had known instinctively what she had missed. But now was not the time for regrets. Now he was here, and he was allowing her to love him as no other man ever had. She trailed her mouth upward to his nipple and favored it with the same loving attention he had bestowed on her, discovering it with her tongue and lips. When she felt his flesh tauten, she leaned over him and kissed his lips, her mouth tenderly fastening on his. He opened his mouth and let her tongue discover the warmth that waited for her. She felt the rising passion that he was curbing in the tension in his body, the way his hands gripped her back and shoulders.

The thud of his heart beating against the bareness of her breasts was another betraying sign of his disturbed pulse rate. Still kissing him, feeling the warmth of his response as he returned her passion, she let her fingers move to the waistband of his pants. He wore no belt, and the snap gave easily. But as her hand brushed the naked skin at his waist, he groaned softly and pushed her hand away.

She pulled away to look at him, a slow, mocking, utterly

121

feminine smile lifting her lips. "Was my kiss satisfactory? Or would you like me to try again?"

He stared at her. "Yes—and yes. My God. You're . . . unreal." He leaned forward and kissed her soundly on the lips, then stood up to strip away his clothes. When he had finished, he lay down beside her. She gazed at the long, male strength of his arms and legs, the well-modeled symmetry of his torso. He was a delight to the eye as well as to the touch, and when he untied the strings on the tiny strip of her bikini and the final barrier between them was gone, she felt only a searing flame of joy.

Now the journey of discovery began all over again. She touched and kissed and caressed him, her sensitive hands learning every contour of him, the roundness of his chest muscles, the hard-corded strength of his back. He was an inviting contrast of textures, smooth sleek skin and crisp hair, strength and male power. At the same time, he explored her with infinite gentleness in his hands. He touched her face, her earlobes, her breasts, her throat, his fingers worshiping the texture of her skin, the soft feminine curves of her. Nothing about her escaped his loving attention. He kissed her knees, her ankles, ran his fingers over the smooth calf of her legs to the sensitive backs of her thighs. He was setting her on fire, making her a trembling mass of sensation, the fur tickling her back, his hands warming and touching every inch, traveling along the smooth thighs—where he found the sweet feminine core of her.

If she thought she had experienced pleasure in his arms before, it was nothing to this. His gentle touch sent its erotic delight shuddering through her until she seemed to be a part of him. Time stopped—and yet whirled around her. An endless aeon went by, her need for him spiraling out of control. She wanted him so much. Her writhing body betrayed her. With a lithe twist, he moved over her and made her his.

"Kaynon—" she murmured his name, and he went very still, as if he were afraid he had hurt her.

"All right?" he asked huskily.

"Yes. Oh, yes—" His heavy weight filled her emptiness. She felt the touch of him everywhere, at breast, hipbone and thigh, even down to the tips of her toes where they rubbed against his hair-rough legs.

As if he knew exactly what she was feeling, he lay still and kissed her face, her eyelids, the smooth flushed skin of her cheek. Then his mouth came down on hers, and he began the slow, sensual rhythm that seemed to worship and claim and possess her body and soul. It fanned the fires within until she exploded with him in a shower of light and color and ecstasy.

Lying beside him, she felt the fur rug brushing sensuously on her back as his arm lay across her waist. She turned her head to look at him. In the soft light of the dying fire, he looked rejuvenated, exhilarated. His skin glowed, his eyes were bright with the knowledge of her. She could only look at him with envy. A sated lethargy kept her locked against his warm chest. He traced a lazy circle around the creamy curve of her breast. The warm tingling began all over again, and she moved in protest. His hand closed over her shoulder with a gentle but commanding pressure. "Where do you think you are going?"

She shook her head. "Home—"

A teasing sparkle made his eyes brilliant, and his vibrant energy reached out and dominated her. "You're not going anywhere."

"I can't stay here all night—"

"Why not?" He leaned over her, covering her mouth with a lazy, drugging kiss. His lips robbed her of what little willpower she had. "You can't go home in that skimpy bikini. You'll catch cold." He brushed his lips over hers, teasing, nibbling.

"Your concern for my health is touching." She strove

123

for a light, bantering tone, but she didn't feel casual. The feel of his warm mouth moving over hers was beginning to be very familiar—as familiar as the melting sensation in her bones his lips induced.

"In fact," he said, "I'm so concerned for your health, I'm going to suggest you take a warm shower."

"Just to make sure I don't catch cold," she murmured.

"What other reason could I possibly have?" His mouth trailed over her cheek, her jaw, her throat.

"I can't think of one." She could think of a dozen, and none of them had to do with her health. Kaynon's reasons had more to do with the renewed passion in that warm mouth that was traveling over her face than any concern for her well-being, but she no longer had the strength to pull away. He was weaving a silken cord around her—and she was powerless to stop him. The idea of picking up her suit and towel and going home, *leaving him,* was intolerable.

He got up and held out his hand. "Come with me."

When she hesitated, he reached for her. Without a shred of self-consciousness, he pulled her to her feet. The brush of her breasts against his chest made her pulse leap, and she knew that the passion she had just experienced with him hadn't been slaked. It was latent, lying below the surface, and needed only the slightest tremor to send it surging through every inch of her again.

He locked her to his side with an arm over her shoulder and walked up the stairs. Her legs moved as if directed by his will rather than hers. She was caught on a riptide, a fast-flowing current that kept her moving in whatever direction Kaynon decreed.

In a bathroom covered with cedar paneling and luxuriant hanging plants, he extended an arm in toward the shower. When he had adjusted the water temperature, he guided her inside, stepped in behind her, and pulled the folding door closed. While she was struggling with the clamor of her senses, he took the soap in his hands, made a lather, and with the supreme self-assurance that was such a part of him, he began to rub her body with the palms of his hands in sensuous, gentle strokes, his fingers sudsing her breasts, her abdomen, her thighs.

Latent fires flared. "Kaynon—"

"Shh." He quieted her instinctive protest. "Don't think. Just feel."

"I—" She wanted to tell him that it was too much, that she was afraid, desperately afraid. She didn't want to love this much again, she couldn't trust herself. But as if he knew exactly what she was thinking, he pulled her into his arms and stopped her words with his mouth, kissing her. She was bombarded with sensual delights, Kaynon's tongue caressing hers, the water pouring over her, the feel of his hard body pressed against her own soap-slicked one. The breath seemed to leave her lungs. She hung suspended over an abyss of sheer delight.

He lifted his mouth from hers and examined her bemused face, a faint smile on his own. He began to cleanse her back, his hands moving down the length of her spine. He found and massaged the sensitive hollow in the same devastating way he had that day on the dock. But now she wore no swimsuit to hinder his exploration of the rounded curves of her buttocks. He took his time, and when she could no longer bear the exquisite intimacy of his hands cupping her bottom, she made a small sound. He understood, and without saying a word, stooped to soap her thighs, her legs, her ankles.

When he finished, he straightened and handed her the soap. "Your turn."

CHAPTER SEVEN

In the brief moment of her hesitation his gaze asked the question he couldn't give voice to, and she saw it again, that hint of vulnerability and need.

She took the soap, made a lather as he had done, and deposited the white bar back in its dish. Facing him, adoring him with her eyes, she started at his shoulders, feeling the reassuring firmness of him under her palms. As she moved lower, over the well-developed chest muscles, the hair-crisp skin transmitted an acute sense of pleasure to her hands. He was warm and real and alive, and his courage to let her touch and explore him made her body sing with delight. She had never known such heady enjoyment could be generated by touching a man. She closed her eyes, savoring the sensations, thinking only of him.

Gently, she turned him under the shower spray and lovingly directed the cascading water over his shoulders, his arms, his torso, rinsing the soap away.

Moments later, after she had dried him with a fluffy towel and he had done the same for her, he guided her gently toward the bed. She stood beside it while he pulled back the covers. When he picked her up and placed her between the smooth sheets, she could only think of how absolutely right it felt to be carried in his arms.

He followed her down, and with a soft groan, his mouth claimed hers. His hands began to caress her, and the passion that lay below the surface flared into a white-hot heat.

Those rocketing sensations began all over again, and she was his once more.

She woke once in the night and heard the song of a bird, a sweet, throaty clashing of notes that together created a haunting beauty. She shifted her position and felt the answering slight movement from Kaynon. He lay facing her. More than anything, she wanted to stay awake and watch the pale first light of dawn touch the interesting curves and hollows of his face. But her lids drooped, and she slept.

She had shifted during the night and now was lying with her back to him, cuddled against him spoon fashion. The sun blazed into the bedroom, and its brightness told her it was not early. With a faint little tingling of alarm, she turned. "What time is it? You'll be late for work."

She gazed up into green eyes that were suddenly alert, gleaming with little yellow lights fanning out from the pupils. "I've decided I'm not going in today." He bent his head and covered her mouth with his. "Good morning."

A shyness and a resounding little bump in the pit of her stomach made her lashes flicker down. "Good morning."

The lazy, taunting voice said, "Sleep well?"

"Yes," she said, still not looking at him. "Your bed is very . . . comfortable."

A hand on her chin forced her face up. "What's the matter?"

"I—nothing," she said huskily.

"I'm glad," he said, giving her a quick, hard kiss. He lifted his mouth from hers, propped himself up on his elbow, and said, "Let's get up. I'm hungry."

She opened her mouth, and he raised his hand and touched her lips. "Don't tell me. I already know you're a disaster in the kitchen. But somehow, between the two of us, we'll have to get breakfast."

"I can make toast and fry an egg."

"Well, that's a relief. I thought you were totally useless." He rolled away from her and got out of bed, his back to her.

She grabbed his pillow and threw it at him. He tossed it back at her casually, but hit her squarely in the face.

"You don't play fair," she said, laughing up at him.

He picked up his robe and thrust his arms into it. He was tying the belt, gazing down at her, his eyes frankly perusing the outline of her breasts under the sheet. She smiled, and he came down on the bed, crushing her back into the pillows with hard hands on her shoulders. "And I suppose you want me to believe that you do."

Her smile was brilliant. "Oh, always."

"Liar." He bent over her, trailing his mouth over the top of one rounded curve. "You haven't played fair from the moment I saw you."

Her thoughts flashed back to the night she met him, and she said ingenuously, "You were annoyed when you thought I wasn't particularly interested in talking to you, weren't you?"

"Did you do it on purpose?"

She was silent for a moment, thinking. "I'm not sure. I . . . suppose I was . . . afraid."

He trailed his mouth along the elegant curve of her throat. "Afraid this might happen?"

She shook her head and laid her hand on his shoulder. "No. I was afraid I might want it to happen."

He raised his head and cupped her face in his hands. "I won't hurt you, Tarra."

A jolt, a fey shudder went down her spine. "Don't say that. It's—unlucky."

He stared at her for a moment, searching her eyes with his own. His mouth curved upward. "What an intriguing woman you are. I thought you were all depositions and dusty law briefs, seasoned with a love for Oriental discipline and self-restraint. Now I find a strong streak of superstition swimming around in that cool, logical mind."

She made a mocking little grimace. "Analysis before breakfast. I can't take it on an empty stomach."

He leaned over her, pressing her back in the pillows, his face mocking, sensual. "Could you take me on an empty stomach?"

She braced her palms against his robe-covered chest. "I thought you were hungry." She knew it didn't make any sense, but in the bright light of the morning sun, the gleam in his eyes made her self-conscious.

He said softly, "Maybe I've decided I'm hungry for you."

He made no move toward her, but simply watched and waited. She stared at a spot over his shoulder and hedged, "I . . . can't do a thing till I've had my coffee."

He chuckled, a low, husky male sound. "Now why did I know you were going to say that?" He pushed himself up off the bed and went to the chest of drawers on the opposite side of the room. "I'll lay out a shirt and a pair of shorts you can wear with this belt." There was a pause. Then he drawled, "I doubt if your suit is dry. I don't think we remembered to hang it up."

He laughed softly down into her pink face and then left the room. She clutched the sheets, listening to the pad of his bare feet on the stairs.

The shirt was too big, but perhaps that was just as well, since she had no underclothes. She threaded the belt through the waistline of his denim shorts, managing to bunch most of the gathers in the material around in the back, and used Kaynon's comb and brush to get her hair in reasonable order before she went down the stairs.

Walking into the kitchen, very aware of her bare feet, she saw the four crispy brown pieces of toast that lay on a plate, already buttered. Kaynon was stirring the eggs around in a stainless steel pan, his brow furrowed slightly, as if it took all his concentration. He looked up, gave her a cursory glance and said, "We'll eat out on the patio. Pour the coffee, will you?"

He divided the eggs onto two plates, poured orange juice, and put everything on a tray. "Can you carry the mugs?"

She nodded and followed him out the door to the redwood deck. The wood was already warm from the sun, her bare feet told her, and a soft summer breeze made the fringe on the round umbrella table flutter.

He put the tray down and set their places at the table, positioning them so that they could look out over the lake. She sat down, not really looking at the rippling, silver-blue surface of the water or the clear, vibrant sky over her head. Out of the corner of her eye she saw tendrils of his dark auburn hair take on the cast of antique copper. There was the added attraction of the whorls of darker, burnished hairs of his chest exposed by the sleeveless vest he wore unbuttoned. His movements made the V-shaped bottom of it ride over the well-worn, faded jeans that clung to his hips and thighs.

As if it would be an antidote to his virile magnetism, she cupped the mug of coffee in her hands and brought it to her lips.

"How is it?" He eased his long length into a chair and stretched his legs out to the side opposite her.

"Excellent. You get a B plus."

He raised a burnished eyebrow. "Only a B plus?"

She laughed self-consciously. "Sorry. That just slipped out. My dad used to give everything that was really good a B plus—never an A. This was in the days before everybody rated things from one to ten."

"You must love him very much." Kaynon asked the question easily.

She picked up her fork and strove for a casual air. "He shared so much of himself with me when I was a child. It would have been extremely difficult not to love him."

The next question came quick as a whipcord. "What about Reece? Did you love him, too?"

She looked at him then, her cheeks warm. "I thought

130

it was women who were supposed to ask men questions after they went to bed with them."

His jaw hardened, but his eyes held hers. "Just answer the question."

"Am I on the witness stand?"

There was a long pause. "Yes."

She laid down her fork, the loveliness gone from the morning. "Don't do this," she said huskily. "Don't make me remind you that you have no right to ask these questions."

The low growl was almost primitive. "Damn it, I do."

"No. One night doesn't give you the privilege to pry into my private life." A sick feeling climbed up the back of her throat, and she pushed back her chair. He caught her wrist. She faced him, tense, her body poised for flight, her eyes glittering. "What now? Do you drag me off to the bedroom and prove your superior strength by overpowering me?"

"I wouldn't have to overpower you," he drawled.

She raised her chin. She felt as if she were bleeding inside. Why were they saying these things to each other? "No, you wouldn't, would you? You've had enough practice to made sure of that. Should I ask you about all the women you've made love to?" She twisted her wrist and tried to get away, but his grip tightened, and his other hand went to the nape of her neck. "Why don't you?" he murmured. "Why don't you give me some sign that you care a little, that I've succeeded in breaking into that cool underground vault you call your mind?" He pulled her closer. "But you don't, do you? I have to keep dropping depth charges—"

The muted ring of the telephone coming from inside the house startled them both. He didn't move a muscle.

It was a way to escape. When he went inside to answer it, she would simply walk down the steps and vanish into her house—and lock the door. "Aren't you going to answer that?"

His eyes narrowed. He gave her a speculative glance, and she had the uneasy feeling he had read her mind. "No."

The phone rang again. She tugged at her wrist. "It might be something important."

"This is important." His eyes flashed over her. She jerked at her arm, feeling frustrated.

"Kaynon, let go of me."

The phone stopped its ringing, and the silence seemed ominous.

"If there's anything antique hunting has taught me," he said in slow, measured tones, "it's the hard fact that when you see something you want, you have to reach out and grab it. If you hesitate and waver, it may disappear into another buyer's hands while you're standing there deciding."

"I'm not an antique," she said coldly.

In the silence, there seemed to be volumes that his hand on her wrist and his eyes on her face were saying. Then a surprising gleam of humor surfaced in his eyes. "That's true." His fingers loosened, and he began to caress the pulse point he had brutalized with his iron grip a moment ago, setting up an altogether different, disturbing tingling on the surface of her skin. "Stay and finish your breakfast."

He wasn't apologizing. But he was asking for a truce, she knew that.

She sat staring at him, feeling that caressing hand rob her of the antagonism, the tension. The probing possessiveness was both a reminder of the passion they had shared and a promise of more to come. A sharp little pang of need arrowed up through her. She moved restlessly in the chair, but none of her effort went toward pulling her hand from his grasp. He watched her like a hawk, and now a smile lifted the corners of his mouth. Dear God, he was lethal. He knew he had won—and he knew exactly how he had won.

"You're holding the hand I eat with," she said crisply, trying not to give him complete victory.

He let her go and relaxed back in his chair, a self-satisfied smile tilting his lips.

Her eggs were cold, but she ate them anyway, knowing she wouldn't have been able to enjoy them no matter what temperature they were. The coffee had stayed warm in the pottery mug, and that, at least, offered some comfort.

He said, "I want to spend the day with you."

The huskiness in the words sent a little jolt through her. He wasn't watching her now, he was gazing out over the water. But it was the vulnerability in the set of his shoulders, the way one hand was wrapped around his coffee cup, the other open on his thigh that captured her. He might have been a small boy looking forward to a day at the park. How did he do it? How did he switch from ruthlessness to sensitive openness?

"Doing—what?"

He glanced at her, and the humor, the quick sexual sparkle was there in his eyes, but his words didn't express it. "Swimming, sunbathing—whatever."

She lifted her shoulders in an indecisive shrug and tried to stifle the butterflies beating at the walls of her stomach. "If that's what you'd like."

"That's what I'd like." The husky firmness in his voice did things to the rhythm of her pulse.

Later, when they had drunk their second cup of coffee, she said, "Would you . . . like some help doing the dishes?"

"No."

She didn't know whether to be relieved or disappointed. Then he said, "I put your suit and towel in the dryer. It should be dry by now."

"Thank you."

His glance flickered over her. "I suppose you'd like to get out of those."

"I'd like to go home and . . . brush my teeth."

133

His smile was lazy. "Why didn't you say something? I have a spare that's never been used."

"It doesn't matter." The need to get away from his lazy, taunting gaze was almost tangible in her bones. "I'll collect my suit and meet you out on the dock in an hour. How does that sound?"

He didn't agree immediately. He seemed to be thinking about it. Then he said, "Mine—or yours?"

"Mine, I think. There's more room—"

His smile mocked faintly. "Yours it is, then."

She was in her bikini again, lying on her stomach and trying desperately to concentrate on her neglected book when she felt the dock shudder in response to his rhythmic step. She had left room for him, and he spread his towel and stretched out beside her on his back, facing her. His muscular, lean body lost none of its attraction in the daylight. Her eyes, hidden behind violet-tinted lenses, were drawn to him almost of their own accord. From her position beside him, she could see the underside of his jaw, the pale patch of skin that was not as deeply tanned as the rest of him. She was swept with a sudden urge to press her lips to that vulnerable spot.

"Book any good?" He lifted his shoulders, shifting to a more comfortable position on the hard boards—a position which happened to bring his hips and legs in contact with hers.

"Not too bad." She tried to focus on the printed page, but the words swam in front of her. Instead, her mind saw his face, the fine lines fanning away from his eyes, the straight nose, the well-cut lips that had kissed every inch of her.

She gave up trying to read and let her head fall forward to rest on the cushion, her face turned away from him.

She felt him move beside her. Alarmed, she lifted herself to face him, but it was too late. His hand pressed her down onto the cushion, and slick with the lotion he had just poured into it, his fingers slid easily between her bikini top and her back. The clip gave.

She made a sound of protest and tried to twist free of his hand.

"There aren't many people out on a Tuesday morning," he said silkily, "but I wouldn't make any sudden moves if I were you." His hand slid over her back, applying the lotion.

"I don't remember this being on the list of things we were going to do," she said, her nerves registering the intimate liberties he was taking with the entire surface of her back, reminding her of the erotic attention he had given her last night.

"You don't?" His voice mocked her lightly. "It was there on the schedule, right before sunbathing and—whatever." His hand went down the length of her spine, hesitated at the top of her bikini pants, slid underneath to caress her curved bottom.

She rolled over, breaking away from that intimate, disturbing caress. "I don't think I'll get sunburned there."

"I can't let you take that chance." But he stopped teasing her and smoothed lotion over her thighs and legs. Those long, expert strokes were no less devastating, and when he calmly picked up the lotion bottle and lay back down beside her, she was relieved. At least she told herself she was.

"You could return the favor." He handed her the lotion and rolled over on his stomach.

"I could, couldn't I?" Her hair blew into the rim of her sunglasses and she took them off and pushed the lock away. She should have hesitated, should have refused, but the memory of the pleasure she had felt touching him and the urge to repay him for his tantalizing caresses of a moment ago ignited a little flame of mischief in her eyes.

She reclipped her top and sat up. Resting her hand on his back, she squeezed lotion into her palm. To keep it from dripping, she cupped her hand and then smoothed

135

it over his skin, imitating his slow stroking, kneading his shoulder muscles and back, carefully keeping her nails from scratching him. His skin was smooth, but underneath that satiny covering, steely muscles and hard bones resisted, rubbed against her sensitive palms. She exerted more energy until she was almost massaging him, running her fingers along the indentation on each side of his spine, probing the little hollow below his waist. Then, as he had done, she inserted her fingers teasingly under the top of his dark trunks. He went very still, waiting. She hesitated, and then probed lower, her palm cupping the top of one rounded buttock. His iron control broke. With a quick, violent motion, he rolled over and grasped the hand she had snatched from under him. His low mutter was almost a growl. "And you say you always play fair." He jerked her forward, bringing her crashing down on top of him. Warmth enveloped her, warm lips discovering hers, warm chest against her breasts, warm sun beating down on her head, warm hands locked on her bare skin, and . . . warm tongue flicking over hers.

She opened her mouth and gave him access to her honeyed sweetness, pressing against him, threading her hands through his sun-warmed hair, feeling the need to get closer, closer. . . . His hands tightened, thrusting her upward, ending the kiss. Hanging suspended over him, she stared down at his hard, sensual face, the dazed hunger still there in her eyes for him to see.

"That's enough, woman." He twisted, forcing her down on the cushion beside him, lifting himself on one elbow to stare down at her, his eyes devouring the sight of her. He picked up a lock of the silky brown hair that fanned out around her shoulders. "Because if you don't want me to make love to you here and now, I suggest you open that damn book and start reading."

Even though the disturbed tempo of his breathing told her he was struggling for control, he let her hair slide through his fingers and moved away to turn on his stomach and direct his gaze out over the water, his eyes narrowed against the sun. She retrieved her book, knowing not a word of it would make any sense, while every nerve in her body waited for the next onslaught on her senses.

There was none. Kaynon lay beside her, his breathing slowing. He wasn't asleep; he seemed content just to lie there and soak up the sun. They lapsed into a quiet companionship. Tarra had even managed to read a few pages when Kaynon shifted to lie beside her on his back. She tensed nervously and looked at him, but his eyes were closed.

The truce and companionship lasted through lunch and an afternoon swim. Kaynon had that wonderful ability to play, and he swam with her, dipping her under the water with a careless hand, fending off her attempts to retaliate, and finally, letting her capture him with her arms around his neck and carry him under the water to give him a sound ducking.

And as she had the night before, she ended the afternoon lying on the rug, shedding her bikini and discovering heaven in his arms.

The glitter of the setting sun on the water danced along the opposite wall. Fire crackled in the fireplace, and two crystal glasses filled with white wine shimmered on the hearth. Kaynon sat beside her on the rug, his hand plunged into the bowl of fluffy popcorn they had prepared together. "Open," he said solemnly, and when she did as he asked, he popped the white nugget into her mouth. His buttery fingers lingered against her lips and her tongue stroked out and licked the fleshy pad. In the firelight his eyes glittered over her. She wore her bikini with his shirt hanging unbuttoned over it, and he caught the edge of it and pulled her close. His kiss was brief but possessive. He wore jeans, as he had that morning, but no vest, and his bare chest brushed her breasts.

When he lifted his mouth from hers, he pressed her

down on the rug and settled his upper body over her soft feminine contours. "Umm, this is comfortable."

"I can't breathe." She couldn't, but it wasn't the pressure of his body that was causing her shortness of breath. Immediately he eased himself up. She lay looking at him from the rug. His eyes gleamed, and then, as if to deny her attraction, with one quick motion he took hold of her arm and pulled her up. "Have some more popcorn to get your strength up."

He extended another white kernel toward her. She hesitated, knowing she was accepting the role of a submissive lover when she ate from his hand. But the submissiveness, the vulnerability flowed on a two-way current. For every time Kaynon extended his hand with a bit of food, he risked her rejection.

She took the popcorn between her teeth and chewed it, watching him. When she could talk, she said, "Am I going to need my strength this evening?"

In the light of the fireplace the pupils of his eyes seemed to leap with flame. "What do you think?"

He pulled her close, his hands finding and exploring the wide expanse of bare midriff her bikini exposed. And at that precise moment, the telephone rang.

"Kaynon."

"Shhh." Even through the crocheted material, she could feel his palm rubbing her nipple sensuously.

"Kaynon, you haven't answered it all day." She remembered Bruce Edwards's call. "Your father may be worried about you."

"I don't need my father to look after me," he murmured, nudging her throat with his mouth.

He didn't have to remind her that he was a mature man. Even now, his mouth was raising havoc with her nervous system. The telephone went again. "But he can't help worrying. He might have the police out looking for you."

He shook his head. "Be quiet, woman." And he silenced

her with his mouth on hers and his heavy weight bearing her to the rug.

The phone stopped its incessant ringing, and there was silence in the cottage—only to be broken by the shrill clang as the phone started up once again.

She struggled under his heavy weight, and her resistance brought a soft curse to his lips.

"If you won't answer it, I will."

He levered himself up on the palm of his hand and sat looking down at her. "Be my guest." The curve of his mouth tightened. "Just be sure you tell whoever it is to go to hell. I'm spending this night with my lady."

She had half risen, but at the husky possession in his softly spoken words, her pulses leapt, and she relaxed back on the rug. In the firelight his jade eyes seemed to claim her as the phone chimed on.

He asked, "Aren't you going to answer it?" The words were low with sexual challenge.

A log collapsed into the fire, sending sparks flying up the chimney. "No," she said softly.

His lips relaxed into a sleek, satisfied smile. "Let's go upstairs."

Wordlessly she held out her hand. Together they walked up the stairs, and when he pressed her down on the bed and stripped her suit away, his mouth and hands made her forget that there was any other world beyond that sensual one that he wove around her.

The next morning she woke in Kaynon's bed, brought to consciousness by the familiar ring of the telephone. She stretched out her hand, looking for him. "Kaynon—"

He was gone, only the warm, male scent of him proof that he had been there. She heard the phone stop abruptly, and Kaynon's deep tones sounding more subdued than usual, as if he were trying to talk without waking her. But as she listened, his tone of voice changed subtly, became strained and harsh. The sound of it made her throw the covers back and climb out of bed.

A vague sense of worry plagued her as she crossed the soft, plush green carpeting. Kaynon's bedroom should have relaxed anyone—it was done in earth tones of brown and green with walnut antique furniture—but somehow she wasn't distracted from her pangs of anxiety. The sun slanted in the narrow windows at the top of the high ceiling. The light was new, yellow, as if the sun had just crested the horizon. It was very early to be receiving a telephone call.

She went into the cedar-walled bathroom to shower and clean her teeth with the toothbrush Kaynon had laid out on the counter for her in its sealed box. When she came out, she felt refreshed, much more awake, and convinced that her worries were the work of an overactive imagination.

She got back into her bikini, knowing that today she would have to go to her cottage and get some clothing. The morning air was too chilly to be running around in her swimsuit. Then she saw the shirt that Kaynon had laid out on the dresser, evidently for her. Made of soft white India cotton, it had long sleeves. She put it on and rolled the sleeves to just below her elbow.

She went down the stairs and found him in the kitchen. He wore his robe, but her eyes were drawn away from the lean attraction of his body wrapped in blue terry cloth to the brooding frown that furrowed his brows, and the hard set of his mouth.

He said abruptly, "I have to go back to the city. There's trouble at the gallery."

"What is it?"

"The T'ang horse has been stolen."

Her rasp of indrawn breath seemed to echo in the quiet kitchen.

"That's the best of it. The worst is that it had to be somebody with access to the keys. There was no sign of forced entry, and the cabinet was still locked when Eric discovered the horse was missing—which means it had to have been relocked after the horse was taken out."

"But who would—"

He gazed at her, his green eyes like pools of jade. "My charming brother thinks I did it."

The blood left her cheeks. "He couldn't. You must have misunderstood him. What possible reason would you have for—"

"How quick you are to jump to his defense," he murmured. When her eyes widened at the unwarranted attack, he said carefully, "He has his reasons, and they are logical —up to a point. He thinks I might have done it to show the need for a more elaborate security system, something I've been pushing for since I cam . The thing that really points it in my direction is the fact that the cabinet was locked after the theft." A mocking half smile played over his mouth. "Eric and I are the only ones who have access to the cabinets."

"That doesn't mean anything," she said staunchly. "Anyone capable of stealing a valuable work of art is capable of stealing a key."

"On the other hand," he went on, watching her, "it occurs to me that if I am suspected, even though I might be cleared later, I would still be discredited. I would find it difficult, if not impossible, to contact people and ask for their support for the gallery. I would be forced to quit my work—and leave town." He didn't flicker an eyelid. "It's possible that's what my brother wants."

"Why would he want such a thing?"

"Because he wants a clear field with you."

If he had struck her, he couldn't have thrown her more off balance. "That . . . can't be true."

He gazed at her from under heavy-lidded eyes. "I didn't say it was true. I said it was a possibility."

"He doesn't love me—"

"But he wants to marry you."

"I've told him no."

"He hasn't accepted your refusal. He plans to continue his—pursuit."

A quick, uplifted turn of the head brought her eyes up to collide with his. "Have you been discussing me with him?"

Not a muscle moved in the hard mask of his face. "The subject came up."

She put out her hand to the countertop for support. It was cool, impersonal under her hand. "So, in case I gave in to your brother's persuasion, you took me to bed."

She waited, praying that he would deny it, unable to do anything but stare at that rock-hard face.

His mouth dissolved into a mocking, sensual smile. "You had a choice." His eyes drifted lazily over her. The thin, gauzy white cotton showed the outline of her full breasts barely covered by her black bikini bra. "This is the second morning you've climbed out of my bed and put on my shirt."

The pain was almost unbearable. Her body cried out for relief—and found it in the heated, numbing rage that raced through her veins. "Well, there won't be a third time, you can bet on that."

She whirled around, but he caught her arm and turned her back. "Is your self-esteem really that low that you think I would go to bed with you just to best my brother?"

"My self-esteem?" she cried. "My self-esteem isn't under discussion."

"Oh, yes, it is. And you're going to need it, because you're not walking out on me now."

She trembled with anger and pride and hurt, uncaring that he must feel the tremors in her body under the hard fingers that clamped around her upper arm. "Watch me."

He didn't release his hold. "I need a lawyer."

She stared at him in contemptuous disbelief. "Try the Yellow Pages."

"And have this story splashed all over the newspapers? No. I've got to have someone I can trust."

142

Her mouth twisted. "That lets me out." She struggled, trying to pull away from him.

It didn't seem possible that his grip could tighten on her arm, but it did. "How do you think my father will feel, seeing this family squabble played on the local TV news?"

She stopped struggling and stared at him, her eyes flashing with temper. "You should be the lawyer. You know exactly which string to pull!" She strove for control, trying to marshal her wildly conflicting emotions into order. Even his fingers gripping her arm made her remember other ways he had held her. "Don't think you can use my affection for your father to whip me in line. I'll find you another lawyer. The city is full of them."

"I don't want another lawyer. I want you."

"Why would you want someone who can't stand the sight of you to represent you?"

He stared down at her, and for the first time, she saw that his breathing was not as regular as it might have been. "Because you're going to be just as interested as I am in keeping this story away from the press."

"You're wrong," she said scathingly. "I hope they hang you."

"If they do," he gritted, "they'll hang you along with me."

"I have nothing to do with the gallery. I have no keys."

"But you're involved with me. And you've been seen around town with Eric. How long do you think it would take some enterprising reporter to come up with a different slant on this odd little burglary? Not another thing in the museum was touched."

"I can't—represent you."

Slowly, he slackened his hold on her arm, his fingers sliding down the inside to the bare skin of her wrist. Then she was free. "Because we've been to bed together?"

She shot him a hot look. "No, because I despise you."

He clenched his jaw. "You don't have to like me. You only have to keep me from getting into more trouble."

"I'm not sure that's possible. You seem to have a natural bent for trouble."

"Not this kind."

She turned, and he said to her back, "You're going to let your emotions keep you from being professional?"

She felt as if she were running on a treadmill. There was no escape from him. Without facing him, she said, "I've only been practicing for a year. You need someone with more experience."

"I don't want someone with more experience. I want you."

Slowly she turned around. "I can't do it." The words were blunt, cool.

He relaxed back against the counter, his dark, hard face not revealing the slightest trace of unease. "You have no right to refuse me for emotional reasons." He paused, and heavy-lashed lids half hid his eyes. "If you were a man, you wouldn't."

Her body tautened. "You use every cheap shot in the book, don't you?"

She had reached him with that. Two dark spots of color burned under his cheekbones. "Damn it, I need you." His words echoed in the kitchen. They vibrated in her brain, bounced around from cell to cell, not as she heard them now, but as he had whispered them to her only a few hours ago in the warm, dark quiet of the night, making her soul melt and her body arch to him.

She hugged her arms around her middle to ward off the sudden feeling of sickness.

He grimaced and thrust a hand through the dark thickness of his hair. For the first time, he looked disturbed. "Damn it, I'm in danger. Can't you see that? I'm fighting for my life. My entire career is built on generating people's trust. If Eric brings charges, I'll be finished. Who wants to give money to a thief?"

"Eric wouldn't do that. He couldn't."

144

"He's already suggested that if the horse isn't found soon, he will."

"Bruce wouldn't allow it."

"My father couldn't stop him. No one could. I'm a prime suspect."

She said, "There would have to be something a lot stronger to point suspicion in your direction than the mere fact that you have access to the keys."

"But it's got to be someone who had a key. There's no other explanation."

She looked at him coolly and knew that she couldn't let him down, no matter what he had done to her. "You won't need a lawyer until you are formally charged. Until that time, I'll act as your legal counsel—only if you agree that if Eric does file charges, you will get someone more experienced and less . . . involved."

He said softly, "I . . . agree."

Why did she feel it was his victory rather than hers?

He said, "Can you be ready to go in an hour?"

"Ready to go where?"

"Back to the city. I want you to come to the gallery with me."

"I hardly think that's necessary—"

"I'm your client. And I say it is necessary."

He was cool and remote and absolutely relentless.

She thought about arguing with him and knew it was useless. She said just as coolly, "All right. I'll be ready in an hour."

CHAPTER EIGHT

It was still early when Kaynon guided his father's car to a stop in front of the gallery. Everything looked normal enough, and somehow, Tarra thought ruefully, it shouldn't have. As if to mock her worries, a wren warbled a joyous song in the oak tree on the side of the house as if to say, what was the matter with her, everything was all right with his world, and the early sun gave the grass and trees a green-gold glow. Kaynon stopped the car on the curved drive and got out. Tarra opened her door, but before she could put her legs on the ground, he was there, helping her out with a hand on her elbow.

The air was cool inside the gallery, the air conditioning already whirring. Tarra, with Kaynon's hand on her arm, walked across the oak parquet floor, the hollow sounds of their footsteps on the wood in the empty room increasing her sense of foreboding. She slid her hand over the wood banister and listened to the stairs creak under the carpet as they climbed to the second floor, telling herself she was being ridiculous. But she couldn't help remembering the times she had felt that way walking into the courtroom with the senior counselor—only to sit and watch him lose the case.

Kaynon pushed open the outer door of Eric's office without knocking. Pamela, the picture of efficiency in a vivid aqua jacket with a white silk blouse demurely tied in a bow at her throat, sat at her desk, and though part of her expression might have been surprise, Tarra got a fleeting glimpse of a violent emotion in those tawny eyes before long lashes came down, hiding a glittering, avid excitement so strong that the sight of it sent a chill over Tarra's backbone.

Her attention was drawn away from Pamela. Through the open door she could see that Eric hadn't risen from his desk, and he, too, wore an almost hostile look. It was only then that it occurred to her how it must look, she and Kaynon together in the early morning hour, Kaynon's tanned fingers hard and possessive against the long sleeve of her warm-pink linen suit.

Kaynon guided her inside the office and shut the door.

Eric wasted no time. "Why is Tarra with you?"

"She's acting as my legal counsel."

Eric reddened, the color giving his pale face an almost artificial look. "That isn't necessary."

Kaynon released his hold on her and pulled a leather chair away from the wall, indicating that she should sit in it. He found another for himself and eased his long frame down, faced his brother, and favored him with a saturnine look. "Wouldn't you do the same if the situation were reversed?"

Their immediate lapse into antipathy made Tarra move restlessly in her chair. "I've agreed to come with Kaynon so that I might ask some questions that may throw some light on the theft," she said coolly. "But if you're going to pick at one another the way you did when you were children, I'll leave you to it."

Her cool words seemed to sober both of them. Eric shot her a smooth, almost antagonistic look. "I suppose Kaynon has told you everything."

"He's told me only that the horse has been stolen and the case neatly locked behind. There are several questions that occur to me. I thought I remembered you telling me you go around and visually check all the exhibits before you leave at night."

"Normally I do," Eric said defensively. "But when Mrs.

147

Stratton-Duncan called around four and sounded annoyed that Kaynon wasn't there, I decided I'd better go see her." His mouth twisted ironically. "As it turned out, she was concerned about our security system and wondered if her collection would be safe here." Long fingers drummed on the rust-colored desk pad and dark eyes stared at Kaynon. "If word of this gets out, she'll certainly withdraw her offer. I've been trying to contact you for two days. You were supposed to be at the lake, Father said. But obviously you weren't." He paused, thought for a minute, and then burst out, "Where the hell were you, anyway?"

Coolly, Kaynon said, "None of your business."

She pulled them back by saying crisply, "I'm not here to listen to your personal arguments. Do you want to discuss the theft or not?"

Both men were silent, Kaynon slumping into his chair, Eric staring at him with the bright spots of color still flaring under his skin.

"Now, you were saying. You left the gallery Monday afternoon around four o'clock. As far as you know, the horse was still there. But you didn't actually see it, is that correct?"

Eric nodded.

"What time did you come back to the gallery?"

"I didn't. I was at Mrs. Stratton-Duncan's for about an hour. Then, since it was after five and I knew Bart would be on duty, I went and got a take-out sandwich and went home—it was around quarter to six, somewhere in there. I tried to call Kaynon at the cottage off and on all that evening. No answer. The next morning I came in and made my usual rounds."

"And that was when you discovered the horse was missing, is that correct?"

"Yes," Eric said coolly. "The horse was missing—and so was my brother. He wasn't at the lake—at least he didn't answer the phone—and no one knew where he was.

148

All I had was the note Pamela left from Monday saying that my father had loaned his car to Kaynon and wanted a ride home, but had gotten tired of waiting for me and called a taxi." He shot another heated look at Kaynon. Kaynon's face was bland.

"But if the horse was gone when Bart came on duty, he surely would have notified you."

"No, not necessarily. At least, I'm not sure."

"You're not sure?" This from Kaynon. "How could you not be sure?"

Eric was belligerent. "Bart doesn't make rounds. He was hired for the sole purpose of making sure the doors and windows are locked after hours and to sleep on the premises in case the alarm goes off. The alarm is supposed to keep anyone from stealing anything."

She asked, "Who turns the alarm system on?"

"It's on all the time, day and night."

"So as well as knowing where the key was kept for the Plexiglas cabinet, the culprit also had to know how to turn off the alarm system."

Eric stared at her. "No, not exactly."

"Not exactly?"

"The alarm isn't activated by a key in the cabinet."

"That means," Tarra said, thankful that her voice sounded cool and impersonal, "that the thief had a key—and knew it wouldn't activate the alarm."

Eric looked miserable. "Evidently."

"Didn't Pamela see anything?"

Eric gave her a blank look. "Pamela?"

"Doesn't she work until five?"

"You aren't—you're not suggesting that you suspect her?" Eric was incredulous.

"No, I'm only saying that she was here."

"Pamela couldn't possibly have done it. She doesn't have access to the keys."

"Never, not even during the day?"

149

"The only two keys for that cabinet are on my key ring and Kaynon's."

"He hasn't worked here long. Why did you give him a key?"

"Because he insisted on having one," Eric said. "He gave the exhibits a thorough examination when he first came, to see if we might be exhibiting something that was a fraud."

"And were you?" She directed the question to Eric, but glanced at Kaynon. He sat silent and unmoving in his chair, his long legs encased in black pants, his buff-colored silk shirt open at the throat. She had to close her mind to the attraction of him, those bronze hairs visible at the hollow of his throat, long, lean legs stretched out in a way that accented his casually sexual magnetism even though he was only lounging in a chair two feet away from her.

"One," Eric admitted unwillingly. "An Oriental ivory statue that failed the needle test. I was so sure, I hadn't bothered to check it."

"So the horse could have been taken anytime between four o'clock Monday afternoon and six o'clock the next morning—providing the thief knew about the alarm system and could avoid running into Bart."

"I guess that's right."

She asked, "What happens when the alarm goes off?"

"It starts a siren and sends a signal to the police."

"Your father was here until four thirty," she said. "Have you told him about all this?"

Eric's eyes were guarded. "No. I wanted to talk to Kaynon first. I thought that if he—if he *had* removed the horse from the case, he could replace it immediately and no one would ever know about it. But now—" he shrugged. "I have a tour group from out of town coming through at ten. They have our catalog, so I'll have to make some sort of explanation about its absence." He looked unhappy. "I suppose I could say it's been taken out of the

150

case temporarily. That's true enough. But if it comes out later that I lied to the public—"

"Let me go talk to your father," Tarra told him. Eric made a sound of protest, but Tarra shook her head. "No, he's got to know, and in addition to that, he was the last one on the scene. He may know something we don't."

Eric frowned and looked even unhappier, but in the end he said, "I suppose you're right." He was silent, looking down at the desk pad. When he raised his head, his face was expressionless. "I might warn you that Dad isn't in the best of humor the first thing in the morning. He was annoyed because he couldn't contact you," he said to Kaynon. "You may not get a pleasant reception."

Kaynon shrugged and made no sign that he was disturbed, but Tarra felt a surge of guilt that nearly overwhelmed her. Kaynon and his father, after years of alienation, had reached a neutral ground and were relating to each other for the first time since she had known them. The last thing in the world she wanted was to be the cause, if only indirectly, of another schism between them. If only she had answered the phone . . .

Bruce Edwards still lived in the lavish, huge house on East Avenue, but lately even he had been complaining about the high cost of heating the Victorian mansion.

They were ushered into Edwards's bedroom by his butler. The drapes were still drawn, but several lamps were lit, giving the room a soft glow, as if it were still evening. Bruce Edwards sat up in bed, a wicker tray in front of him. The tray held the remains of his breakfast. A napkin was tucked into the collar of his brown silk pajamas. He held a huge brown mug in his hand, which Tarra supposed contained the remnants of his morning coffee. Edwards had, like his son, been an actor in his youth, and he had come very close to making it his career. He hadn't lost his flair for the dramatic, Tarra thought ruefully. The bed was a huge old walnut four-poster, the doweled posts stabbing the air, the coverlet a plush purple, and on the wall above his head frowned a Scottish ancestor in full regalia—kilt, bagpipes, collies, and all. On the bedstand beside him sat a portrait of Kaynon and Eric's mother. She had been the one to give Kaynon his auburn hair. Her copper-colored tresses framed a beautiful oval face and eyes of the same startling green as Kaynon's.

Kaynon seated Tarra in a comfortable chair next to his father. He seemed seized by a restlessness, however, and wandered over to pull a drape and look out the long, narrow window. "You keep this place like a mausoleum," he muttered. "Why don't you ever let any air in?"

"Maybe I'm just getting in practice for my afterlife," his father returned wryly.

"Don't give me that." Kaynon's voice was gruff, hiding his emotions. "You'll outlive us all."

"That's not possible," he blustered, his tone betraying the fact he wished it were true. "Did Eric tell you I was trying to reach you last night? Where have you been?" Without giving him the chance to reply, which was fortunate, Tarra thought, he turned to her. "Tarra, my dear, you're a refreshing sight for tired eyes at this hour of the morning. Can I have Alfred bring you some coffee?"

"No, thank you, we—that is, I've already eaten."

Bruce shot a look at his son, still standing at the window, and then fastened his gaze on Tarra. His dark blue eyes, as piercing as Kaynon's, narrowed on her. "Are you two coming to tell me something that will make an old man happy? Is there going to be a wedding in this family, finally?"

Inwardly she cringed. Hectic color flowed in her cheeks. She smoothed her linen skirt over her knees and hoped her blush wasn't noticeable in the soft light of the room. Behind her, Kaynon said nothing. He was leaving it all to her. "No—no," she said quickly. "It's something—something has happened at the gallery, and we thought you might be able to help."

"The gallery?" He frowned, immediately distracted

from his thoughts of matrimony. "What's the matter with the gallery?"

"A work of art has been stolen, the T'ang horse."

"Impossible," he said at once. "I saw it there Monday."

"You definitely remember seeing it when you left?" Tarra asked carefully.

"Of course I do. Had damn little else to do, waiting for Eric, so I went around to all the exhibits, trying to imagine myself a visitor for the first time. Hard to do, but it can be done. I saw all kinds of things we need to change."

"But the horse was there," Tarra said insistently.

"Of course." He stared at her as if she weren't quite bright. "Need to display it against dark cloth, velvet maybe. Contrast the hard, shiny glaze against the soft fabric."

"What time did you leave the gallery?"

"It was four thirty. I remember telling that gal, Eric's secretary, to leave him a note. She did, didn't she?"

"Yes, she did." Tarra sat back, thinking. "So at least we know it wasn't taken during the day on Monday. It had to be after four thirty."

"Was that the only thing taken?" Bruce Edwards asked.

Briefly she explained, telling him about the cabinet being locked after the horse was taken.

"Damn strange." Bruce Edwards looked beyond her shoulder to the still figure of Kaynon, standing by the window. "You got any ideas, Son?"

"No." The word was cool, blunt.

The older man's discerning eyes turned back to Tarra. "What's your part in all this, young lady?"

"I'm—" she stopped, not wanting to go on. It would hurt him to know that one of his sons had accused the other of stealing.

"She's acting as my legal counsel, Dad," Kaynon said coolly.

"Legal counsel? Why? Are you being accused? You couldn't possibly have done it. You've been at the lake."

153

In a blinding flash, she thought *and with me. He was with me Monday night, all day Tuesday, and Tuesday night. He couldn't possibly be involved,* she thought—and was ashamed to feel relief pouring through her. She shouldn't have had the slightest doubt.

"You don't need legal counsel," Bruce blustered, his face slightly tinged with red.

"I suppose that's true," Kaynon drawled. "Now I'll have to look for another excuse to keep her with me."

The lazy sensuality in the words disturbed her, and she hardly dared look at Bruce Edwards to see what his reaction was. But he seemed to find nothing out of the ordinary about his son's extraordinary statement, and went on asking questions about the gallery, which Kaynon answered. Bruce expressed his desire that Kaynon explore methods of enacting tighter security measures.

Kaynon straightened away from the window. "Maybe you'd better take that up with Eric."

Bruce Edwards blinked and looked astounded, as if he had forgotten he had another son. He reached for the telephone beside his bed. "I'd better call him, caution him not to let the news leak to the papers." He shot Tarra a calculating look. "Was there anything else you wanted to ask?"

"No," she said, rising. Kaynon came to set the chair aside and said, "I'll get your car back to you as soon as I can."

Bruce blustered and dialed Eric's number at the same time. "You're welcome to use it as long as you need it. I won't be using it."

Once he had made the decision to go, Kaynon was anxious to be away. They said their good-byes quickly and walked out into the sunshine. The contrast between Bruce Edwards's darkened bedroom and the midmorning summer sun made Tarra blink.

"Dad loves a stage," he murmured sagely as he helped her into the car.

She could only think of what willpower and determination it must have taken for Kaynon to pull away from the domination of his father.

He started the car and pulled out into the street. "Would you mind coming with me to the gallery where I'll pick up the battery from my car and take it to the station to get it charged?"

"Is this another excuse to keep me with you?" she asked pertly, not sure if she was taunting him or hoping he might agree.

He turned his head. Green eyes flickered over her in a quick, caressing glance. He had his own ways of dominating, she thought ruefully, and she would never be free of his spell.

He didn't withhold the answer she craved. "Yes." The soft word made her heart soar. Was he finding that he needed her as much as she needed him? The thought brought a heady pleasure. Then he said with a cool practicality that destroyed her euphoria, "I need someone to drive Dad's car back to his house when I've got my own running," leaving her to wrestle with the hurt his cool words inflicted as he drove down the tree-shaded street to the gallery.

After Kaynon removed the battery, they had trouble finding a station. The first one was too busy, the second had others ahead of him with the same problem. They ended up driving down Monroe Avenue and were almost out to the suburb of Pittsford before they found a station that could begin charging the battery immediately. Since the process took almost two hours, Kaynon suggested eating lunch in the Old Mill while they were waiting.

Tarra had been there many times before, lunching with Eric. Those times seemed pleasant compared to this one. Kaynon was silent in the car, and now, as they climbed the stairs and were shown to a table by the window that overlooked the Erie Canal, he seemed to have lapsed into his taciturn mood permanently. He gazed out the window,

155

and she knew he was watching the paddle wheel rotating slowly, water pouring downward, pushing the paddles with sheets of cool blue-green liquid.

When asked by the waitress if she cared for a cocktail, she shook her head. Kaynon did the same. "Bring us some coffee."

They were left alone, and Kaynon went on staring out the window, a brooding frown creasing his forehead. She was not up to making polite conversation, either. She sat back in her chair and let the silence build between them. Kaynon was thinking, turning something over in his mind, the theft perhaps, and after the interview with his father, she didn't have the strength to carry the burden of the conversation on her shoulders.

They ordered, and when the waitress left, Tarra said coolly, "You are cleared of suspicion, you know that, don't you?"

His eyes left the wheel, flickered over her, looked blank. "What are you talking about?"

Struggling to keep her voice level and impersonal, she said, "You were on your way to the lake when the horse was stolen, and you've been with me ever since."

He didn't seem to be surprised. "Which leaves us with only one other culprit."

"Eric?" She shook her head. "There's got to be some other explanation."

Their appetizer, the Mill's famous cream-filled clam chowder, was set in front of them. Steam rose from the center of the heavy crockery bowls.

"Your loyalty is commendable."

It was the second time he had intimated that she felt something for Eric, and it annoyed her. She dropped her spoon on the small plate under the bowl and flashed him an angry look. "I'm no private investigator, but I do know that it's simply not compatible with Eric's personality to take a work of art from his own gallery. There's too much at stake. Mrs. Stratton-Duncan had just told him how

156

apprehensive she was about the gallery's security for her collection—"

"Which gave him the idea of the perfect way to sabotage my work."

Tarra shook her head. "No. The status of the gallery will soar once those paintings are hung on its walls, and Eric wants that to happen more than anybody."

"Then we're left with no suspects."

Tarra dropped her eyes and became very interested in the creamy texture of her food. "There are one or two other people who had the opportunity to help themselves."

"Who are you suggesting might have done it? Pamela? Bart? Dede?"

"I don't know. I'm merely saying that all the possibilities haven't been exhausted yet, and you have to keep an open mind," she smiled faintly, "especially in front of a blank wall. I'm hoping perhaps your father will come up with something more. He was the last one on the scene."

"You don't think he did it." The words were dry, mocking.

She was impatient with him now. "No, of course not. He had no motive."

"You may not call yourself a private investigator, but you're beginning to sound like one."

She gave him a cool look. "You may think the idea of 'motive' is overworked, but it is a sound principle. People have reasons for the things they do, and to them that reason is logical, even though it might not appear so to someone else."

"But the whole thing goes back to the keys. No one had a key but Eric and me."

"But if someone else used a key to open the case, then someone else had to have a key. The sooner you accept that fact, the sooner we may find the culprit."

"Wax copies?" he said wryly, lifting an eyebrow.

She shook her head. "That's some writer's overworked

imagination. There is no process that copies a key out of wax. The only way to copy a key is to do it with a machine —which is an easy, cheap process that's readily available."

"But you have to have the original to make a copy."

"Yes, of course. Which means that at some time recently your keys—or Eric's—were out of your possession . . . long enough for someone to make a copy."

He seemed to be thinking about that. "I suppose that's possible. In fact—" his brow puckered as if he were trying to remember, "Eric lost his not too long ago."

She picked it up at once. "He lost them? When?"

Kaynon looked at her and grimaced in exasperation. "I don't know, last week maybe."

"How long before he found them again?"

"He didn't. I gave mine to Pamela to copy for him—"

She dropped her spoon, the click of it against the edge of the heavy bowl reverberating through the room. *"You did what?"*

He stared back, his eyes a hard, glittering green. "I'd forgotten all about it till just this moment."

Something chill crawled over her spine. "How strange that you could forget something like that."

His eyes narrowed. "Don't you believe me?"

"I—I don't know." She went on eating her chowder, but the bitterness in her mouth seemed to have stolen the flavor.

"Do you think I'd deliberately withhold the information?"

"Perhaps you were . . . protecting her—subconsciously, at least."

He was silent for a moment, and then his mouth twisted into a thin line. "Maybe I was—especially since you're determined to go around accusing everyone."

She had no reply to that. After his censure of her, nothing she put in her mouth was palatable, and she still tasted the bitterness of jealousy and mistrust when they left the Mill and climbed back into the car to drive to the station. Once they were there, she tried not to watch the lean litheness of Kaynon's body as he crossed the concrete apron to talk to the station attendant, but she couldn't tear her eyes away from him, and she was glad when he disappeared inside and she could no longer see him. When he returned, holding the battery, he slid under the wheel of the big gray Mercedes-Benz, and she could smell the faint, clean smell of him, and that well-remembered scent made her nerves clamor with need.

He stared at her for a second or two and looked as if he were going to say something, but he didn't.

As he drove back to the gallery, she watched as his dark auburn hair blew around his head in the breeze, and the memory of how she had threaded those coppery strands through her fingers made her mind cry out in pain. How could he have forgotten about Pamela's taking his keys—unless he cared for her? And yet, to be fair, she supposed it was something that had happened briefly in the routine of his day and had little significance at the time. At least that's what she told herself. Was she grasping at straws?

Kaynon pulled the big car into the gallery parking lot and stopped the motor. Tarra got out with a sense of relief while Kaynon replaced the battery in his car. Kaynon opened the door of his gray Volks and said roughly, "Get in, I'll go in and leave the keys to my father's car with Eric and then I'll take you back to the lake."

She would have protested if there had been any other way to get to the cottage, but there wasn't, so she got in, determined that she would make it through the hour drive without revealing her inner turmoil.

When he got back in the car, nothing was said and he remained distant and remote for most of the trip. She watched the countryside fly by, a green and luxuriant countryside bright with rays from a sun that had delivered on its early-morning promise of heat. She wished she could take off her jacket, but she forced herself to leave it on. It was very little protection from Kaynon's sharp eyes, but it was protection.

By the time they reached the lake, she was feeling the heat. Perspiration trickled down her back, making her silk blouse stick to her skin. The shade of the trees and the cooler air felt heavenly on her face as she opened the car door. Dancing flecks of silver played over the water, making it an inviting sight.

"What are you going to do now?" he asked as she got out of the car.

"Go for a swim," she said, and walked down the hill, not looking back, not letting her mind register how he hadn't made a move to follow her.

"Enjoy yourself?"

She had just come into the kitchen thinking dispirited thoughts about trying to fix herself something to eat, when she saw him. He startled her. He hadn't rapped. He was standing on the patio just outside the screen door, watching her. In the late afternoon heat he wore only a pair of denim cutoffs, his chest bare. She was in her damp suit, padding around in bare feet, not wanting to change because the wet material would keep her cool.

"Yes, I enjoyed myself," she said shortly, still hurting. "Did—did you want something?"

His hair was damp from his swim, the swim he had taken as soon as she got out of the water. An hour ago, tired of swimming, she had climbed out and walked down the dock away from the lake—only to see him stroll to the end of the dock and plunge in. He had purposely avoided being in the water when she was, and that had hurt. She wasn't about to fall all over herself asking him to come in.

He opened the screen door and stepped inside, and the small kitchen got suddenly smaller. "You haven't eaten, have you?"

She thought about lying and gave it up, knowing he could see for himself that she hadn't. "No."

"I'm fixing something for myself. Care to join me?" His eyes flickered over her, mocked her hesitation. He had to know how torn she was. She hated to prepare food, even for herself.

"I—all right. I'll just change and come over."

"You don't have to change." The lazy challenge was there, daring her to remember the last time she had come to his house wearing only her swimsuit.

"I'd rather get into some dry clothes," she said coolly and walked out of the kitchen, leaving him there to let himself out the door.

She got into a brown prairie skirt and a loose cotton blouse. It was a muted gold color, and it brought out the little gold streaks in her dark brown eyes. She fought to keep her composure while she combed her hair, knowing she would need every scrap of it when she walked across the lawn and climbed the patio stairs to Kaynon's cottage. She was almost sure now that Pamela had taken the horse and that Kaynon believed she had, too, but he was unwilling to admit it—to her, and probably to anyone else as well.

She slipped on comfortable sandals, spent more time than she really needed on her makeup, and told herself she was ready. There was nothing left to do but go.

He answered her knock promptly, and when she stepped inside, his eyes flickered over her. He had changed, too, and wore a pale cream silk shirt with dark brown pants. He made no comment, but simply led the way to the dining room. He had set the table as lavishly as he had the night he had entertained Mrs. Stratton-Duncan, only lacking Tarra's candles, and he seated her in the place of honor at his right and proceeded to serve her an omelet that was fluffy and tasty, full of cheese and peppers and onions. There was toast, too, cut in thin strips and seasoned with herb butter. He poured white wine into the delicate crystal, and when she sipped it, she discovered it had been chilled to just the right temperature.

Her lack of appetite at lunch and her swim had combined to make her very hungry, she realized when he offered her a second helping of omelet and she accepted it.

At the end of the meal he poured the coffee, handed her the steaming mug, and said, "Go on in the living room. I'll stack the dishes and join you shortly."

She did as he suggested, not wanting to subject herself to the domesticity of doing the dishes with him. There was no fire in the fireplace tonight for her to watch, so instead, she looked out the broad expanse of glass at the play of light over the water and sky that formed colors of lavender, gold, blue, and rose. He came to join her, carrying his coffee cup.

The vista out the window shimmered. Outlined against it, he settled himself cross-legged on the rug where they had made love, and the glimmer in his eyes told her he knew what she was thinking. She was jolted into saying prosaically, "Thank you for dinner. It was excellent."

"You are welcome," he said just as formally and brought the cup to his lips, his eyes holding hers over the rim. "When will you be going back to the city?" He drank a bit and then set the cup down carefully on the hearth.

"Saturday probably. Unless it rains. Then I'll leave sooner."

"May I call you from the city tomorrow night?"

"Of course."

His eyes met hers. "Suppose I need you. Would you come in Friday?"

She made a restless movement on the couch and set her cup down on the low glass table. "Kaynon, I think it's time we stopped playing games with each other. You won't be needing me as your legal counsel. You have an ironclad alibi."

"I do?" His dark eyebrow lifted in the familiar mocking arch.

"Yes," she said bluntly. "Me. I can vouch for the fact

162

that you did leave the city at four o'clock, because you arrived here around five. And . . . I was with you for most of the time after that."

"You think Pamela did it?"

"Yes, I think she did it. She had access to the keys, and she had a motive." She hesitated. "Everything . . . fits."

"What motive?"

"She . . . wanted to hurt you."

He gave her a wry look. "Maybe I deserve it."

"Do you?" The two words were crisp, dry. "Why? Because you denied a spoiled little girl something she wanted?"

"No. Because I kissed her, danced with her—to get at you." He reached out and ran a fingertip up along the bone on the outside of her bare leg. The caress was unexpected, shocking, and set off little explosions under her skin. Slowly the fingertip ascended, pushing aside the ruffle of her skirt. "So, you see, I am responsible." He leaned forward and feathered a kiss over her knee.

That he could talk about being responsible for Pamela and bestow an intimate caress on her at the same time sparked an explosion of her temper. She jumped off the couch and cried at him, "Good. Be responsible. Be responsible as hell. I'm sure she'll be grateful—and find an appropriate way to express her gratitude!"

She was almost to the door when he caught her. A hard hand on her arm whirled her around. "You're not going anywhere."

Her face hot, her breathing quick, she said furiously, "Oh, yes, I am. I'm clearing out to make room for the next candidate for your bed."

"This is no damn election," he growled, and covered her mouth with his.

It was all there in his mouth for her to have, that curious combination of passionate command and gentle persuasion that she had dreamed about but had never known until Kaynon. His tongue probed, his mouth wooed, his hands pressed her closer, molding her against him, making his need evident. She made a soft sound in her throat, knowing he was swamping her senses, knowing that if she didn't move away now, she wouldn't be able to. She tried to push him from her, but he shifted one hand up to her nape, and there was no escaping the total, mind-drugging whirlpool of his kiss. She recognized her body's subtle changes to accommodate the harder contours of his, the clutch of her hands on his back, and knew that her responses must be telling him she was weakening.

He lifted his mouth.

"Kaynon—"

He cupped the back of her head and held her against his chest. "Unless you're going to say something appropriate —like 'I love you'—don't say anything."

She stood in shocked silence, trying to think. How could he ask her to declare her love to him when he cared nothing for her?

"You can't do it, can you? You can't say those words to another man because you still love Bryant. But you can't deny what we have together—"

"I don't love Bryant—" The floor seemed to shift and move under her feet. He was guiding her toward the stairs.

"Don't lie, Tarra, please don't lie to me." He caught her chin in his warm hand, gave her a hard kiss, and then turned her around. His hand on her back was pushing her forward, and her foot automatically lifted to step on the first stair. "At least let's keep things honest between us. You may not love me, but you want me physically. That's enough for now—I'll make it enough." His voice roughened. They were in his loft bedroom, and in the twilight the room was shadowed, hazy, like a secluded bower in a fragrant forest.

"Kaynon—"

He kissed her to stop the words, and his fingers found and loosened the tie at her waist. Half of her blouse fell away, and he quickly found the snap that kept the other side secured. When she would have protested, should have protested, his fingers pushed the sleeves from her shoulders and the garment slid to the floor.

She wore a lacy, flesh-colored bra, and he traced along its low-cut scalloped edges, making her skin in that super-sensitive area tingle with delight. When her low moan told him of her response, his fingers found the front clip, and that garment, too, drifted away to the floor. Her skirt quickly followed, as did her bikinis. She stood before him, naked but strangely unself-conscious, for there in his eyes was a world of emotion—admiration for her feminine beauty, and his own male need to possess that beauty. Yet he didn't move. He waited in utter stillness, waited for her to move toward him. That small part of her heart still guarded against him capitulated. She was his in whatever way he cared to have her. Slowly she raised her hands, and with loving care she unbuttoned his shirt, letting her fingers caress his chest on their downward path until all the buttons were free and she could ease his shoulders out of the material and toss it away. His eyes never wavered from hers as she unclasped his pants and ran the zipper down, letting them fall to the tops of the soft moccasins he wore. She knelt to slip them off his feet. She rose and slid her hands under the waist of his last brief garment, and as she drew it down his legs, a harsh, almost strangled groan escaped his throat. He clasped her to him and half fell with her onto the cool sheets.

"I've been waiting for this," he breathed, cupping her breast in his warm hand, trailing his other hand down the smooth, graceful line of her body from midriff to thigh, "aching for this," his fingers at her breast circled the rosy peak that quivered in taut eagerness, "living for this," he leaned over her and took her nipple in his mouth, playing with it with his tongue, sending depth charges of want and need rocketing through her. "I need you too damn much," he nipped the sensitive bud gently as if to punish her. "Tell me you need me, too, even if you have to lie a little."

"I need you," she whispered huskily, and because she knew he didn't believe her, she said it again, in a throaty murmur, "I need you very badly—" her words ended in a gasp as his hand wandered lower and discovered her navel, circled it, and wandered lower still to that dark and secret center of her feminine body.

Lovingly, he caressed and pleasured her, discovering new ways to delight her. His mouth at her breast was a torment, tantalizing, teasing with its promise to possess the rosy crest but not quite doing so. As if he were tasting every inch, the slow, erotic drag of his tongue explored the full curve, coming close with its torturing promise and then sliding away before the promise could be fulfilled. She was caught on a precipice, wanting the lovely agony to go on and yet aching for his quick possession. She clasped his back and ran her hands over warm skin already satiny with perspiration, loving the feel of him under her fingertips. He favored her other breast with the same erotic caress, and when she thought she would die with wanting him, he took the rounded center into his mouth and explored its burgeoning fullness with his tongue. She smoothed her hands over his hair, soft little moans escaping her throat as she threaded its crisp, vibrant strands through her fingers and urged him closer, closer. She explored his back, the elegant curve of his spine as he bent over her, the sinewy strength under the smooth skin of his shoulders, the hipbones that were so close to the surface of his skin she could trace their curves. While his body was giving her intense tactile satisfaction, his mouth and hands were submerging her in a flood of sensual ecstasy.

She moaned in protest, her body crying out for him.

"Yes," he breathed, "yes. Want me, Tarra. Want me the way I want you—" His harsh words ended in a savage sound of torment that made her heart soar, and he moved over her, filling her mouth with his tongue and her emptiness with his male strength.

She dissolved into a sense of heady rightness, of being

complete. This was where she belonged, here, with Kaynon, her body joined with his, her movements guided by his hands, her legs intertwined with his. His passion was relentless, driving, primitive, and that was exactly what she needed—a mindless tide of passion to swamp her, to make her forget that she didn't belong to this man whose body possessed hers so ruthlessly. He was demanding, compelling her response, and she lost what few inhibitions she might have had left and moved with him, climbing up and up until she fell from a great distance and exploded into that ecstatic, radiant world only lovers know.

She lay beside him. He reached out to touch her breast, and she flinched, knowing that her body was still shuddering with aftershocks, knowing what his touch could do to her even now.

In the twilight his face twisted with pain and his hand fell away. "I was a brute. I can see why you wouldn't want me to touch you." When she might have protested, might have explained, he said roughly, "I think you'd better go home."

Oh, God, they had been so close and now they were worlds apart. He didn't understand her, and she couldn't explain because he wouldn't believe her. What good would an explanation do, anyway? He wanted to be rid of her. He had sated his passion, and he had had enough. From ecstasy, the plunge to despair was quick and chilling. "All right," she said, the words almost catching on the sickness in her throat as she rolled out of bed and snatched up her clothes to escape into the bathroom.

CHAPTER NINE

The humiliation of dressing with trembling fingers, of putting clothes on the body that had known his hands and mouth on every inch, nearly choked her, but somehow she managed to get into her clothes and emerge from the bathroom. He was wearing his blue terry cloth robe and leaning against the dresser, a drink in his hand, his face shadowed, utterly unreadable in the light. He looked cold, icy with anger.

"Kaynon, I—"

He raised the glass in a mocking salute and said evenly, "Get out of here, Tarra, before I decide to take you to bed and keep you there till I get you out of my system." The words were evenly spaced like tiny flicks of a whip, cool and icy with contempt, and he accented them by putting the glass to his mouth and draining the amber liquid down his throat.

"Kaynon, please listen to me—"

He set the glass down on the dresser with the care of someone who is extremely angry. "The jury's out, counselor, and court is closed. The judge refuses to hear your appeal."

"If you'll just listen to me—"

He walked toward her then, slowly, and in that slowness was silent, menacing threat. "God damn it, go, Tarra."

She went, half stumbling down the stairs, pride keeping the tears from spilling out of her eyes.

* * *

She didn't sleep well, but toward the early morning hours, she finally dropped off into a light doze. She knew she hadn't slept long, and when she heard the violent pounding, she thought at first it must be coming from inside her head. It wasn't. It was coming from her front door.

It was Kaynon, of course, it had to be, and the thought that he wanted her so urgently he was shaking the house with the repeated pounding of his fist made her heart race, jarred the nerves that had been relaxed in sleep. She threw on a short, silky robe and ran down the stairs. Without thinking, she pulled open the inside door. He stood outside on the patio, just as he had last night, but this time his face was pale with anger.

"Let me in." There was such cold command in his voice, she stepped aside. He looked as if he would tear the door off the hinges if she didn't.

"It didn't take long, did it? Your boyfriend works fast, doesn't he?"

"I don't know what you're talking about—"

He slapped the rolled newspaper down on the counter. "I'm talking about Goodson's column."

"Peter? What about Peter?"

"You're surprised?" he jeered. "But then, maybe you weren't quite sure he could get it into this morning's paper. Well, he did. He must have sat up all night writing after you called him. And you did call him after you left me, didn't you? Because I know damn well you didn't talk to him when we were in the city."

"I don't know what you're talking about—"

"This should clarify things for you." He pointed to a place in Peter's column about halfway down. She forced her eyes to focus and began to read. "A call to Eric Edwards, curator of the family gallery at 100 East Avenue, today confirmed the rumor that was relayed to this writer that a work of art has been stolen from the Treasures of

169

the Orient collection at the gallery. 'We're not quite sure how it happened,' Mr. Edwards said. 'It may be an internal problem. We're working on it.' When asked if the police had been notified, Edwards admitted they hadn't. More questions brought out the fact that the stolen work of art was a valuable authentic T'ang horse, worth well over one hundred thousand dollars. The horse is small, about sixteen inches high, and could be easily sold or smuggled out of the country to be offered on the legitimate antique markets in Europe or Asia. Oriental artifacts from the T'ang dynasty are always in demand. When questioned on the whereabouts of Edwards's brother, Kaynon, the dynamic fund-raiser who is currently working at the gallery, Eric would only say that his brother lives out of town and couldn't be reached for comment. Other sources revealed the key to the theft is, in fact, a key. The horse was taken from a locked cabinet with the use of a key. After taking the horse, the culprit relocked the cabinet, a sort of unique reminder of the futility of locking the barn door after the horse is stolen. Our sources tell us that there is an alarm system at the gallery, but that it is not activated on the use of keys in cabinets or doors."

She raised horrified eyes to him. "Yes," Kaynon agreed and glowered at her, "now the whole world knows about our antiquated security system, thanks to you."

"I . . . had nothing to do with that article."

"Who else would have? Who else knows everything that 'another source' told Goodson?"

"I . . . didn't."

He stared at her. "You wouldn't have had to do this, do you know that? You had me on my knees. I need you so damn much I was going to ask you to marry me, even though you still carry Reece around inside your head like a burr."

Anger—hot, searing, cleansing anger—boiled through her brain. He didn't know her at all. If he could stand there and accuse her of all manner of vile things and then

170

say he was going to marry her, he certainly didn't love her. "Well, what a lucky thing this happened. Now you've been spared."

"I haven't been spared anything. You've left me nothing." He pivoted and strode out of the room, leaving her reeling with the violent self-loathing she had heard in his voice.

Two days passed, two long dreadful days, their dreariness unmitigated by the fact the sun shone and the water was warm. They were dreary because the house next door was empty, empty of the man who had stolen her heart. There was no pleasure in lying out on the dock or submerging herself in the silky water. Too many memories rose up to haunt her, too many husky murmurs of passion lingered in her ears. Desperately, she kept busy, cleaning, swimming, jogging. But he was there inside her brain, and he wouldn't leave.

The last afternoon, she got into her white maillot, grimly determined to lie out in the sun and stop the churning thoughts that roiled through her mind. She picked up her book, when her eyes fell on her portable radio. She had purchased new batteries before she left, thinking it would be pleasant to listen to music out on the dock. Now it would be more than pleasant; it would be vital to her sanity. She gathered it up along with her towel.

Out on the dock she spread her towel and lay down. There was only one radio station with enough power to reach the lake, and she switched to that one and lay back and closed her eyes.

For almost a half hour she drifted in a mindless daze, blocking Kaynon out of her mind. Then, at the end of the hour, the news came on. She was only partially listening—until two words, *Edwards Gallery*, riveted her attention.

". . . T'ang horse has been found, according to Bruce Edwards, the owner of the gallery. He claims his younger son, Kaynon, discovered the precious work of art wrapped in a brown paper bag in the trunk of his car." She sat bolt upright, her hands clammy with perspiration. "No explanation was given as to the reason for the horse's disappearance. 'We won't be filing charges,' Mr. Edwards said, even though he admits he has been advised that the theft should be reported to the police. There is some speculation that his unwillingness is related to an alleged charge lodged by another employee that Mr. Edwards's younger son, Kaynon Edwards, is responsible for the theft."

She breathed in sharply.

"The younger Edwards has agreed to answer questions during a press conference scheduled for three o'clock this afternoon—"

The wild flailing outward of her arm as she scrambled upward knocked the radio over and sent it skittering close to the edge of the dock. She caught it just before it fell into the lake. With hands that shook with her urgency, she gathered her towel and sandals, only to drop one.

Her "damn" carried out over the water and probably was heard on the other shore, but she wasn't in the mood to worry about such trivial details. If she ran into the house, changed, and drove at top speed back to the city, she could be there in time to be with him at that news conference.

Heat waves radiated from the city streets. She jockeyed her car into a tiny spot three blocks from the gallery, got out, slammed the door, and ran toward it, cursing herself for wearing high heels.

There was already a man from the television station there, a portable camera slung over his shoulder. Several other men and women milled around in the main part of the gallery, some of them looking at the paintings, others hardly able to hide their avid eagerness.

She walked across the oak floor and was greeted by a burly figure guarding the stairs. "Sorry, miss, no reporters allowed in the office area."

172

"Bart, my name is Tarra Hallworth. I'm Mr. Kaynon Edwards's legal counsel, and it's imperative that I see him now, this moment."

He squinted at her. "You know who I am, but how do I know you are who you say you are?"

"Well, you can relax. If I'm not, Kaynon will toss me down the stairs." Her mind mocked silently, *He might anyway.*

Bart, heavy and red-cheeked, chuckled in a way that moved every part of his upper body. "Reckon you know Mr. Kaynon all right. Okay. You go on up."

They were all in Eric's outer office, Kaynon, Bruce, Eric, Dede, Pamela.

"What's this nonsense about you having a press conference?" she asked without preamble, looking only at Kaynon.

Kaynon sat with one leg on the desk, but now he straightened and faced her. He had never looked more like a buccaneer pirate than he did today in a jade-green silk shirt and dark pants that were taut across his powerful thighs. "What are you doing here?"

"In case you've forgotten, I'm your lawyer."

"I don't need a lawyer. I'm terminating your services—as of now.

"If you go down there and talk to the press," she said crisply, "you're going to need all the help you can get. Do you realize how much trouble you can get into by saying the most innocent thing?"

"I certainly do," he murmured, holding her eyes with his, a gleam of sensual remembrance lighting the little yellow sparks in his eyes.

"Call it off," she said bluntly. "They'll pulverize you."

"I'm not inexperienced in dealing with the press."

She made an exasperated sound. "Not in a situation like this."

Bruce Edwards moved in his chair. "It was my idea to

173

have a press conference, Tarra. I thought it would clear the air."

"Oh, sure, it will clear the air. It will also clear Kaynon's life of his career." Bruce subsided at once, his face sober, unhappy.

Eric, standing behind his desk, said, "Don't you think you're overreacting a little?"

She stared at Eric. "All right," she said coolly, her head turning back to Kaynon. "What are you going to tell them?"

He said, "I'll tell them the truth."

"The truth? That you were out of town when the horse was stolen, and that it was a coincidence you couldn't be reached for twenty-four hours after the theft because you weren't answering your phone and it was also a coincidence you found the horse in your trunk?" She stopped to catch a breath. "That sounds perfectly plausible to me," she said caustically. "I'm sure everyone will accept your airtight explanation without question."

"Well, counselor," the emphasis was heavy, "what do you suggest I do?"

"Call off the conference. Sit down with me and I'll help you prepare a statement that will protect your rights—to be released to both the papers and the television and radio stations at the same time. Then wait for speculation to die down. It will, eventually."

She waited, her eyes and face pleading with him to consider her words. There was silence in the office. No one seemed to breathe or move.

At last he said, "No, Tarra. I can't do it. If I call off that conference now, the public will believe I'm guilty, no matter what kind of legalese you conjure up to protect me."

That cut her as nothing else could have. She felt the color drain away from her face and her knees buckle.

Bruce Edwards interjected, "Son, maybe Tarra's right. If we wait—"

His jaw hardened. "I'm not waiting. The conference goes on as scheduled."

She stole a glance at Pamela then, and something about the woman's expression surprised her. She had expected her to look triumphant. Instead, she looked stunned—almost dazed. Dede's normally rosy cheeks were pale. She moved toward Tarra. "Can I get you a cup of coffee? You can wait upstairs with us while—"

She wanted nothing more than to fly from the room. Kaynon had rejected her as a woman and as a lawyer. How much more could she take and still walk around? Her legs seemed to have turned to rubber.

"What time is it?" Kaynon asked abruptly.

"Five minutes to three," Eric told him.

"Here, drink this," Dede said, handing her the cup.

She took it, her cold hands clutching the warm cup. She took a sip.

"I'm going down," Kaynon muttered. "Get it the hell over with."

She couldn't just stand there and watch him walk to his own execution. "I'm going with you." She handed the cup back to Dede.

"You damn well aren't," he growled savagely, and inwardly she quailed, but outwardly she kept her face emotionless. "You can't stop me—unless you throw me down the stairs and give them a better story than even they dreamed of bringing back."

He opened his mouth to say something and then closed it. He clamped his hand on her arm and guided her toward the door. "All right. If you're determined to go with me, we'll go down together." When they were out in the hall out of earshot of the office, he said to her in an undertone, "but if you have some quixotic idea of saving me by telling them you were with me—you can forget it. I don't want your help."

She paled. His cruel words were like fine rapiers probing the most sensitive parts of her body. He was determined

175

to shield Pamela, and if he hurt her, Tarra, doing it, he didn't care.

There was the lift of heads and the adjusting of tape recorders and pens over pads as he made his appearance. His grip on her arm carried her to the bottom of the stairs. There he loosened his hold and strode alone to the center of the area they had used for dancing the night of the reception.

"Good afternoon, ladies and gentlemen." He was at once charming and virile, magnetic and compelling. "I'm Kaynon Edwards, and this is Tarra Hallworth, my legal adviser. I'm here to answer any questions you might have about the theft of the T'ang horse."

Her eyes lifted, and at that moment she saw Bryant walk in the door. He motioned for her to come to him, but she shook her head. She stayed where she was, next to Kaynon.

"Is it true that a key was used to take the horse from the cabinet?"

"Yes."

"Your key."

"My key, my brother's key—or a copy of one of those keys."

"Where were you when the theft occurred?"

"I was on my way to Lake Conesus. I've been living there temporarily."

"The theft happened on Monday—but you knew nothing of the loss until Wednesday morning, is that correct?"

"That's correct."

"Where were you during that twenty-four-hour period?"

"I was at the cottage."

"But you couldn't be reached by telephone."

His smile flashed out. "I wasn't answering it."

"Was anyone with you?"

He hesitated. "No comment."

"No comment?" This from an older man. "You mean

there *was* someone with you." His tone took on a sly amusement. "A woman, perhaps?"

"No comment," he said, and smiled, charming them.

"Another twenty-four-hour period went by before you found the horse, is that correct?"

"Yes."

"And where were you during that twenty-four-hour period?"

"Here in the city and at the cottage."

A woman drawled dryly from the back, "Were you answering your phone then?"

Several of the men laughed. "Yes," Kaynon said coolly.

"Peter Goodson stated in his column that his source hinted you and your brother disagreed on certain points of administration here at the gallery."

Kaynon shrugged and that half smile tugged at his lips. "We're brothers. We do disagree—on certain points."

"It was hinted in that same column that you might have taken the horse to point up the need for a better security system in the gallery."

Kaynon riveted the man with a glittering gaze. "If I were capable of hatching such a stupid idea, I certainly wouldn't admit it."

The man bridled instantly. In a slow, challenging drawl he said, "You wouldn't admit it if you'd stolen the horse, either, would you?"

Kaynon refused to be drawn. "The fact remains that I didn't."

"Didn't you do summer stock at one time in your life?" the same woman who had spoken before asked.

Inwardly Tarra groaned. They had done their homework, and she could see where that question was headed.

Unfortunately, Kaynon didn't. "Yes, but I don't see what that has to do with—"

"As an actor, you're certainly aware that a dramatic incident is a far more effective tool to change someone's mind than mere discussion."

Kaynon didn't hide his annoyance. "I wasn't aware of that." His dark head bowed slightly. "Thank you for pointing it out to me."

The woman's face flushed with embarrassment. The tide was turning against him. He was losing them. "What about those mysterious twenty-four hours after the horse was stolen," asked a man who had not spoken before. "If you were with someone, surely that person's verification of the fact would clear you of any involvement in the theft."

The older man who had been abusive mocked, "Yes, Mr. Edwards, if you were with a woman, you can tell us. We won't tell anybody—not even her husband."

There was general laughter. Kaynon's face was pale with rage. "No comment."

"I doubt if this lady has a husband—she probably doesn't even exist."

More laughter. Kaynon's hands clenched at his sides. She tensed, knowing he would not take much more baiting. Bryant frowned and shook his head. Suddenly she knew why he was here. He was here to warn her that if she said a word in Kaynon's defense, her job would be in jeopardy. Carson, Reynolds, and Taylor was an old, established law firm, and they would not like their junior lawyer involved in a front-page story that bordered on sensationalism.

"So in all actuality," speculated the man whom Kaynon had annoyed, returning to the attack, "you may have gone to the lake, come back in the middle of the night, removed the horse from the gallery, stowed it in the trunk of your disabled car that was conveniently sitting in the parking lot, drove back to the lake, and simply waited for your brother to discover that the horse was gone."

An appalled silence fell over the group, and Tarra knew that it was the point of no return. If they walked out of the gallery believing that, there would be no salvaging Kaynon's reputation or his career. Any retraction that might come later would be buried inside the newspaper on page three. All the public would remember would be that Kaynon Edwards had stolen a work of art. Beside her, Kaynon seemed frozen in a block of icy anger.

"That is possible, isn't it," the man prodded.

She stood silent, torn by indecision. She couldn't bear to see him ripped apart like this, but if she said anything, he would hate her. Her choice was clear. She could stand by and see him continue to protect Pamela at his own expense—or she could speak and lose whatever little affection he had for her.

"No comment." She saw a muscle move on the side of his jaw and knew what control he was exerting to confine his speech to those two harmless words.

"It's not only possible," the man who was baiting him said, "that's exactly what happened, isn't it, Mr. Edwards?"

She could feel the anger emanating from Kaynon's body. He was on the verge of losing that tight hold on his hands and mouth. She couldn't stand it any longer. "No—" she cried, and was startled by his sudden fierce grip on her hand. She shook it off and went on. "No, it isn't possible," she said clearly, and she had their attention then! She took a deep breath and went on coolly, "I was with Mr. Edwards from the time shortly after he arrived at the lake Monday night until Wednesday morning when we learned of the theft. He could not possibly have stolen the horse."

There was a short, collective gasp followed by a buzzing murmur. The TV camera swung to her, along with the brilliant lights. Flashes exploded in her eyes as cameras went off, taking her picture.

"Are you saying you are Mr. Edwards's lover?" There was a feline sound of satisfaction in the woman's voice.

"I'm saying I was with him Monday night, all day Tuesday, and Tuesday night and that I can absolutely, without a doubt, vouch for the fact that Mr. Edwards did not leave his cottage during that time except to swim."

"Why didn't you say something earlier?" the man who had baited Kaynon growled.

"Mr. Edwards had asked me not to. He was—" she took a breath and prevaricated, "he thought it might be embarrassing to me to admit that we were . . . together. But I'm not ashamed of the fact. He's a fine man, dedicated to the arts and to making them available to more people."

"Spare us the commercial," the man muttered.

Her temper flared and she swung on him. "No, I'm not going to spare you," she cried. "This is a press conference, and information is supposed to flow two ways. If you don't like what I'm saying, that's too bad. It's your job to report it all, not just the part that happens to suit you."

He held up his hands in mock defense. "Hey, don't bring out the heavy artillery, lady. I'm just doing my job—"

"That's debatable," she snapped.

Kaynon had hold of her arm again and he was cutting off the circulation. "I'm sorry, but we are out of time. Ladies and gentlemen of the press, thank you for yours."

Into her ear, he murmured, "If you say one more word, I'll strangle you."

There was an excited babble of questions. "But I wanted to ask—Is it true that—If you didn't take the horse, who did?"

Voices fired inquiries frantically at them, but Kaynon's decisive stride pushed them aside. His iron grip propelled Tarra through the group toward the stairs and escape.

"Tarra." Bryant was there at the foot, Bart's stolid figure holding him back.

Kaynon hesitated and then said, "Let him through, Bart. He's—a friend of Miss Hallworth's."

They walked up the stairs together, and at the top Bryant said to her, "I want to talk to you. Where can we—"

180

"Use my office," Kaynon said easily, and unlocked the door on the left side of the hallway. Casually, as if she were a package he wanted to get rid of, Kaynon handed her off to Bryant and then walked down the hall—to the office where Pamela was waiting. He opened the door and didn't look back.

She watched him go, fighting the urge to run after him and throw herself in his arms and beg him to forgive her.

Bryant pushed the door closed. "You idiot. You know what you've done, don't you? I came as soon as I heard about the press conference, but I was too late, wasn't I?"

She sank down wearily in Kaynon's swivel chair and pressed her hand to her forehead. Suddenly she had a blinding headache. Bryant always had to set the stage. He could never say anything without a preamble. When he talked to her, she felt as if she were in court, listening to him address the judge. "Just get on with whatever you have to say, would you?"

"You're out of a job," he said bluntly. "Old man Carson was adamant. He warned me that he didn't want to see your name linked with Edwards's in any way, shape, or form. And you've just told the entire city you're his lover."

"So?" She lifted her shoulders wearily. "Shoot me at sunrise."

"Tarra, it isn't a joking matter."

She looked at him then. He was totally correct in his dark suit, pale blue shirt, conservative navy tie. The exact opposite of Kaynon. "Bryant, I appreciate your coming here, I really do. But right now, I'm too tired to care. I—lost some sleep the last two nights—"

"I gathered that," he said dryly.

She grimaced. "I'm sorry if I've caused you any embarrassment," she said wearily. "I'll hand in my resignation on Monday."

He looked at her, and there was a light of admiration in his blue eyes she had never seen there before. "Tarra,

181

I—" his voice softened. "I envy him. He's brought out a hidden . . . something . . . in you that I never could."

"Thank you, Bryant. I . . . appreciate that."

He stood staring at her for a moment and then shifted his feet. "I'd better get back."

"Good-bye, Bryant."

He hesitated, started to say something, thought better of it, and instead said softly, "Good luck, Tarra."

She didn't go back to Eric's office. She couldn't have borne seeing Pamela in Kaynon's arms, a happy smile on her face. She descended the stairs and went out to her car, aware of the heat hitting her in waves from the cement. She would go back out to the cottage for the weekend and try to think what to do.

Cool, silky water slid over her arms. She swam mindlessly, trying to forget the pain, her dark head moving between the blue water and blue sky in a lake dotted with boats: sailboats, catamarans, and powerboats. The hot, clear weather had brought people from the city, people looking for relief from the heat, and even though it was twilight, the water, whipped into waves by the boat traffic, churned over her head and arms. She ignored it and swam back and forth parallel to the shore, exerting herself to exhaustion. For almost a half hour she moved through the water, until the sun went lower in the sky and she began to feel the effects of her marathon swim. Her arms felt heavy, her legs didn't want to move. She would have to get out soon. She forced herself to swim another length, hoping to get a second wind, but she was so tired she could hardly lift her arms up. Conceding defeat, she swam to a shallower depth and stood up.

Wearily, she began to walk toward the dock, feeling her way carefully, not wanting to step on a stone or a clam. As she got closer, a dark shadow on the dock rose to its feet—a shadow holding a towel.

Equal parts of shock and delight raced through her,

dissolved her fatigue. She walked steadily forward, taking slow, deep breaths. At the bottom of the ladder she pushed a wet strand of hair out of her eyes and said, "What are you doing here?"

"Come up and I'll tell you." Kaynon's low voice was so beautiful, so dearly familiar.

Her feet seemed to slide on the rungs of the ladder. When she lifted herself to the dock, she stood for a moment, looking at him. His face was shadowed in the twilight, even his eyes were hidden. She said, "Aren't you . . . angry with me?"

"Furious." But he didn't sound it. The low voice was dark and faintly husky. It went straight to her head. "Is that why you ran away?"

She shrugged. "There didn't seem to be anything to stay for."

"I don't suppose there was—not after you'd told half the city we sleep together." His voice had a droll, amused sound. He gave the towel an impatient shake. "Come here, woman."

The possessive tone made her heart soar. "The last time I did that I ended up spending the night with you."

"Exactly." He waited.

Her heart thumping, she walked into his waiting arms. He swathed her in the terry cloth, his hands rubbing impersonally over her back and shoulders. "What are you doing, training to swim the Channel?"

"I thought I was trying to forget a love affair."

He turned to her, and with a hand at her back, prodded her to start walking down the length of the dock ahead of him. He said nothing to deny her words, and her elation collapsed. She had misread him. In despair she started toward her cottage. He said, "Wrong way. You're coming with me."

She went, her heart hammering as they climbed the stairs and he opened the door for her. When they were inside, he closed the door and pulled the drapes over the

183

expanse of glass. The room became very intimate—and very full of Kaynon.

"What are you doing?"

"Shutting the world out. I've had enough of it for one day." Gently he unwound the towel and took her in his arms. She protested. "My suit is wet—"

"So take it off," he murmured. "I'll help you."

His hands went to the clip at the back of her bikini bra.

"Kaynon, wait. I've got to know what happened this afternoon. You told me you didn't want me to say anything at the press conference. And when I did, you . . . walked away. I . . . thought you were angry with me."

"I asked you not to tell the world about our being together because I thought what we shared was so right, so good, I didn't want it to be fodder for public gossip. I wanted to keep you safe—a part of my life away from the press. But you were so eager to divulge the details of our private life, I thought it must have meant nothing to you."

"It meant everything to me. But your reputation was at stake."

"I didn't understand that—before the press conference. Afterward, I did. You knew what would happen. I didn't. You were magnificent. I was proud of you."

"But you left—"

"The final test. I thought if Bryant still wanted you, I'd give him his chance." He looked down at her with a mocking, amused, slightly arrogant smile. "By that time I was sure you'd refuse him."

"Why—why were you so sure?"

"No woman stands up to a hostile group like that and champions a man . . . unless she feels very deeply about him. After the press conference I knew you loved me—" his hands locked behind her back as if he never intended to let her go—"just as much as I love you."

She tried to conceal the searing delight his words gave her. "What about . . . Pamela? I thought . . . you were protecting her."

184

He sobered. "I did feel responsible, you know. She has problems, and I knew that when I kissed her at the party. I used her to get at you, and I felt guilty as hell. When I went back to the office this afternoon, she admitted the truth in front of Eric and Bruce—that she took the horse and put it in my car and leaked the news to the press. She really didn't want to harm me. Even she didn't realize how much publicity it would stir up. In the end she was frightened. She thought she'd be sent to jail. Dad told her he won't press charges if she agrees to get professional counseling. She really isn't a criminal, you know. If she was, she would have sold the horse and taken the money and run."

He leaned forward to kiss her. She dodged away. "What about the Stratton-Duncan collection? Has the gallery lost it?"

Kaynon shook his head. "All signed, sealed, and to be delivered—as soon as Eric installs a new alarm system and hires two more guards."

He bent toward her, but she stalled him, saying, "How did you know I was here? For all you knew, I might have gone with Bryant."

"I stood up in the widow's watch and waited. Those five minutes seemed like an eternity. God, was I glad to see him come out and get into his car alone!" For a moment, remembering, his eyes darkened. She nestled closer in his arms, and his mouth curved into a self-satisfied smile. "He never had a chance, did he?"

"Arrogant man." She lifted her hand and caressed his cheek.

"Brazen woman," he said, kissing her eyelids. "Now that you've announced our affair to the world, do you suppose you could announce our engagement?"

"I could—if one existed." She flashed a brilliant smile at him. "Does it?"

His drawl was slow, mocking, while his mouth feathered little kisses over her eyes, her nose, her cheeks. "I thought you could at least make an honest man of me."

"I can't." Her fingers went to the button of his shirt.

He pulled away. "What do you mean, you can't?" His voice rose.

She shrugged, pretended blissful unawareness, and went on unbuttoning his buttons. "I can't afford you. I'm unemployed."

The relaxation of tension in his muscles was obvious. "No, you aren't. You've just been hired by Edwards Company."

She frowned, and he looked pleased that it was she who was disconcerted now. "Edwards Company?"

"I'm forming a company, dear heart, that will specialize in fund raising and capital drives for nonprofit organizations."

"I didn't know you could."

"I've been in Buffalo, talking to a man who owns just such a firm. He employs six people, and they all make a comfortable living—nothing elaborate, but comfortable."

"What would my position be in this company?"

"Vice-president, legal counsel—and wife of the president."

"Are you sure I can handle all that?"

"Oh, yes," he said smoothly. "You have all the right qualifications. With your knowledge in the art field, you're tailor-made for the first job. Your logical, clear-thinking mind qualifies you for the second . . ." He paused, and then a mocking, amused smile played over his lips and danced in his eyes. "And your wildly passionate lovemaking qualifies you for the third opening."

She was unperturbed. She looked up at him, her eyes sparkling with laughter and love. "Think *you* can handle all that?" She had reached the bottom button and was pulling his shirt free from his pants.

"Oh, yes," he murmured, and kissed her in a way that proved he could.

COMING
IN
AUGUST—

Beginning this August, you can read a romance series unlike all the others — CANDLELIGHT ECSTASY SUPREMES! Ecstasy Supremes are the stories you've been waiting for—longer, and more exciting, filled with more passion, adventure and intrigue. Breathtaking and unforgettable. Love, the way you always imagined it could be. Look for CANDLELIGHT ECSTASY SUPREMES, four new titles every other month.

NEW DELL

CANDLELIGHT
Ecstasy Supreme

TEMPESTUOUS EDEN,
by Heather Graham.
$2.50

Blair Morgan—daughter of a powerful man, widow of a famous senator—sacrifices a world of wealth to work among the needy in the Central American jungle and meets Craig Taylor, a man she can deny nothing.

EMERALD FIRE,
by Barbara Andrews
$2.50

She was stranded on a deserted island with a handsome millionaire—what more could Kelly want? Love.

NEW DELL

CANDLELIGHT
Ecstasy Supreme

LOVERS AND PRETENDERS,
by Prudence Martin
$2.50

Christine and Paul—looking for new lives on a cross-country jaunt, were bound by lies and a passion that grew more dangerously honest with each passing day. Would the truth destroy their love?

WARMED BY THE FIRE,
by Donna Kimel Vitek
$2.50

When malicious gossip forces Juliet to switch jobs from one television network to another, she swears an office romance will never threaten her career again—until she meets superstar anchorman Marc Tyner.

When You Want A Little More Than Romance—

Try A Candlelight Ecstasy!

Desert Hostage

Diane Dunaway

Behind her is England and her first innocent encounter with love. Before her is a mysterious land of forbidding majesty. Kidnapped, swept across the deserts of Araby, Juliette Barclay sees her past vanish in the endless, shifting sands. Desperate and defiant, she seeks escape only to find harrowing danger, to discover her one hope in the arms of her captor, the Shiek of El Abadan. Fearless and proud, he alone can tame her. She alone can possess his soul. Between them lies the secret that will bind her to him forever, a woman possessed, a slave of love.

A DELL BOOK   11963-4 $3.95